Latasha and the little red TORNADO

A novel by **Michael Scotto**

Illustrations by **Evette Gabriel**

Midlandia
Midlandia Press
Beaver, Pennsylvania

The author would like to give thanks to Jane Price, Kellie Hamilton, Amy Hercules, and the rest of his colleagues on the Lincoln Interactive team. Without all of your support, this book would not have been possible.

Midlandia Press
An imprint of NNDS Corporation
1000 Third Street
Beaver, Pennsylvania 15009
All rights reserved.

Visit us on the web at http://www.midlandiapress.com.

Edited by Ashley Mortimer
Typography by Kent Kerr

ISBN-13: 978-0-9837243-0-8

Library of Congress Control Number: 2011931640

2 4 6 8 10 9 7 5 3 1

Printed in the USA.

First printing, November 2011.

To the fox and the hound

TABLE OF CONTENTS

CHAPTER ONE
THE DOG SWITCH

Momma told me that there is a time in a puppy's life—right around its second birthday—when it just starts to get it. The puppy starts to listen to you all the time and not just some of the time. She stops crying for food under the table and just patiently waits for a scrap. She realizes that yes, her tail actually is part of her body, and no, she'll probably never catch it. Basically, the puppy stops being a puppy and becomes a dog. Momma said it happens very quickly, like someone flipped a switch in the animal's brain.

I wish someone would hit that switch for Ella.

Ella is my puppy. She turned two a few months ago—five months, to be exact, back in April. We don't know the day she was born, just the month, because we got her last year from a rescue shelter for stray dogs. I like to think she was born on April first, because that makes her my April Fool.

That's what I tell people when they ask what kind of dog she is. "She's an April Fool," I say. That will just have to do. I don't know what breed of dog Ella really is. Momma calls her a little red mutt. She isn't mean about it; it's just the truth.

Dr. Vanderstam—that's our vet—he said that Ella looks like dogs used to look six thousand years ago, way back before there were different breeds. I like that because it means that Ella's not just one thing. She's a mix of a whole lot of things. I guess that makes her sort of like me.

I named Ella for my favorite singer, Ella Fitzgerald. You might not have heard of her, but she was famous a long time ago. My puppy's full name is Ella Fitzgerald Gandy, because she is a real part of my family, the Gandys. I only use her full name when she does something bad, though. I think I picked that up from Momma. She does the same thing with me.

When I leave my books all over the living room floor, or if I flush the toilet while Momma is in the shower, her voice gets deep and serious and she calls out, "Latasha Esther Gandy!"

I've really been trying to be good, though. Honest, I have. And not just because I hate hearing my middle name—which I do! I'm trying to be good because I'm not just some little kid anymore. I'm eight years old. That's halfway to being a grown-up.

You know, there's a more grown-up way to say "grown-up." It is called being *mature*. I learned it from my pocket dictionary.

That's what I want to be—mature. I want to be mature for Momma, because she is looking for a new job and she needs my help. And I want to be mature for Ella. If I set a good example for her, maybe that dog switch will turn on and she'll finally settle down.

I'm doing a pretty good job at being mature. Momma hasn't had to call my full name in almost three weeks. I can't say the same about Ella. I use her full name a lot.

"Ella Fitzgerald Gandy!" I cried. It was the day after Labor Day, a sunny September Tuesday, and we were standing on the sidewalk in front of the house.

I had just gotten home from the after-school program at Cedarville Elementary. I just started third grade there last week. I was about to take Ella for a walk down the block. But Ella had another idea. She wanted to eat some of Mrs. Okocho's daisies.

Mrs. Okocho is our downstairs neighbor. She comes from a country called Nigeria. That's in Africa. She is quite elderly—which is a nice way of saying *old*. Momma says it's rude to call people old.

Ella was standing with three paws in the flowerbed and one on the pavement. "Get away from there!" I hissed, glancing nervously in the first floor window.

In most ways, Mrs. Okocho does not act old, or elderly, or even like a grown-up. She has a loud, high-pitched laugh that sounds like a kid being tickled, and a silly sense of humor to match. But there is one thing, and one thing only, that she is deadly serious about: her flowers. She grows them in a big flowerbed in front of the porch. Her favorites are her daisies. They are light purple with tight petals that make me think of an opened-up muffin wrapper.

Maybe that was why Ella had chosen to lick them as if they had a treat hidden in the stem.

"Come on, girl," I pleaded in a low voice.

I was thinking of Ricky Jenkins and what had happened in the summer. Ricky is a boy in my class who lives across the street from me.

Back in July, Ricky was outside playing driveway basketball with his friends. Mrs. Okocho had been out sweeping the porch. Ricky lost control of the ball and it rolled across the street, right into the flowerbed. Mrs. Okocho yelled so loudly that the boys just ran inside without even trying to get it.

I can't quite tell you what she said to Ricky. Some of it was in Yoruba, her home language. And the part that was in English…I don't think I'm allowed to repeat those words.

Ella was standing right where Ricky's basketball had landed. But I wasn't only afraid of getting yelled at.

Mrs. Okocho is more than just our downstairs neighbor. She is also our landlady. She owns the house that we live in on South Graham Street. Her husband passed away a long time ago, and she rents us the second floor of the house to make money. I never wanted Ella to do anything that would make her upset, because Mrs. Okocho doesn't much like my pup even when she is being good! It makes her nervous how Ella always jumps to say hello, and she absolutely hates Ella's licking. Ella licks everything—faces, hands, shoes.

And now, daisies. I shook Ella's leash so that her dog tags would jingle. Finally, the pup looked at me, her ears pinned back in curiosity. I gave her a wide-eyed stare that I hoped said, *Bad dog!* But Ella did not get the hint. She went back to licking the daisies' petals, her tail whipping happily behind her.

Even though she was being naughty, I could not help but smile. I just love watching that pup's tail fly. She doesn't really wag it. It's more like it wags her. It is thick and really long, and when it wags, the whole back half of her body flops like a goldfish out of water.

Suddenly, I heard a sound that almost made my heart stop. It was the scrape of a window opening. My eyes jumped back to Mrs. Okocho's window, but it was still closed. Then I heard Momma's voice from above.

"Latasha Esther Gandy!" she said sternly. I frowned at Ella. There went my three-week record. I looked up and saw my mother leaning out of our living room window.

"You keep that fool dog out of her flowers," she warned.

"I'm trying!" I replied. "She's not hurting them anyway. She's just sniffing them."

And licking them, I added in my mind.

"If you want to argue, young lady," Momma said sharply, "then you can both come inside and have no walk at all."

Big loss, I thought. *You won't even let us walk past Coral Street.* But I didn't say that. I knew why Momma was snapping at me.

This summer, Momma took a class to be a nursing aide. A nursing aide is sort of like a special helper for nurses. Most people call it a CNA, which is good because that fits much better on a nametag. Momma thought it would be easy to get a job as a CNA. Pittsburgh, the city where we live, is jam-packed with hospitals. But it's been over a month now, and Momma is still stuck at her old job as a hotel cleaning lady. It has made her a bit of a grouch lately.

So, I did the mature thing. Instead of arguing I said, "I'm sorry, Momma. You're right."

"That's more like it," Momma said. "Now take her down to the corner and back. I'll be watching."

I made Ella's tags jingle again. "Come on, dogfish, let's walk," I said. "If you're good, you'll get a Teddy Snack." In an instant, Ella hopped away from the flowers. She trotted down the street, pulling me along with her powerful legs.

Ella is not a great listener, but *Teddy Snack* works like a magic trick. Or a light switch.

CHAPTER TWO
ELLA AND THE ZOOMIES

Ella has this weird thing that she does. Well, to be honest, there are a lot of weird things about Ella. Like how she is afraid of our digital camera and of the sound our oven timer makes—and how she's not afraid at all of stinkbugs. But this, I think, is the weirdest thing about her.

About twice a day, Ella goes absolutely bonkers and sprints around the whole apartment. I mean rocket ship fast, like a blur of growling fur. She lowers her body close to the ground and dashes in and out of every room, over and over. After a few minutes of total madness, Ella stops in the living room and basically falls over with a thud, totally wiped out.

She started it this past winter. The first time I saw it, I thought my puppy had lost her mind. I thought she'd gone crazy and we would have to give her away, or at least buy her special medicine for her brain or something. I was so worried that I called Dr. Vanderstam myself. The address and phone number for his clinic are printed on the back of Ella's dog tags.

He told me that Ella's weird habit was not actually that weird. Most dogs do it. It's a way they like to burn off their extra energy. It even has a name. It's called *the zoomies*.

Even though I know it is just the zoomies, I still think it's strange. But it doesn't scare me anymore. Sometimes I turn it into a game. I pretend that I am an announcer at the raceway and Ella is a little red race car peeling out around the carpeted floor.

But not today. Today I was working on important business. Momma had a job interview and she asked for my help to get ready! So while Ella got out her afternoon zoomies, Momma and I just stayed in her bedroom with the door closed.

Momma pulled a pale gray blouse from her closet and held it up in front of her t-shirt. "How about this?" she asked.

"It's too *blah*," I replied. "How about the light yellow one?"

"Good call," she said, sliding hangers aside.

I love helping my mother pick out her outfits. It makes me feel like we're a team.

There was only one thing that would have made me feel better. So I decided to bring the subject up one more time. "Momma," I began sweetly. "If you let me stay up here with Ella, I could do a load of laundry."

"Nice try," Momma replied, checking her yellow blouse for wrinkles. "Anyway, I thought you liked spending time with Mrs. Okocho."

That's right. While she was off at her interview, Momma wanted me to ditch my puppy and go downstairs to get babysat like some toddler.

"Yeah, maybe when I was six," I scoffed. "But I'm eight now. That's a whole extra one-third of my life older."

"A whole third?" commented Momma.

I could tell that she wasn't taking me seriously, but whining about that would not help. "I could use the carpet-sweeper, too," I offered. It was actually already my job to clean up after Ella's fur. I just figured it couldn't hurt to offer instead of being told.

"No arguments, miss," Momma said, all business. She laid the yellow blouse on the bed next to her black slacks and jacket.

"We're not arguing," I insisted. "We are negotiating."

Out in the living room, the growling and sprinting stopped and I heard a thump. I guessed Ella's zoomies were all through.

Momma raised her penciled eyebrow at me. "Mothers and daughters do not negotiate," she said. "Mothers speak and daughters listen."

Except when it comes to picking out blouses, I thought sulkily. *Then mommas ask and daughters tell.*

Momma must have read my thoughts on my face, because her stern expression fell away.

"Mrs. O isn't that terrible, is she?" she asked. That is what Mrs. Okocho told me to call her. She probably thinks that I'd say her full name wrong or something.

"She treats me like I'm still in kindergarten," I huffed. "I am a young lady. I don't need a babysitter."

"Fine," Momma remarked with a shrug. "Then she won't be your babysitter."

I looked up in surprise. Had I actually managed to get my way? "Really?" I asked.

"That's right," Momma assured me. Then a little grin spread on her face. "She'll be your young lady sitter."

That must have been her idea of a joke. I found it not funny at all!

Momma lifted my chin with her fingertips. "Try to be a good sport, sweetie," she said. "I need your help."

I smirked, but then nodded my head. "All right."

"You are an angel," Momma said, and she kissed me on the crown of my head. "I've got to get dressed."

I trudged out of the bedroom and closed the door behind me. I was getting double-frustrated. I was unhappy with Momma for thinking I was too young to stay upstairs alone. And I was unhappy with myself for pouting about it like a little kid.

Ella must have been able to feel my sour mood. When I came into the living room, she was curled into a tight round ball on the couch. She does that when she is nervous. It makes her look like a cute red furball with big brown eyes.

The sight did cheer me up a little. "I know, girl," I said, plopping down next to the pup. I rested my head on her hind leg like she was a pillow. "And the day started out so great, too."

It really had. It all began at breakfast. I like Saturday mornings for a lot of reasons, but a big one is that I get to have breakfast at home.

During the week, I have to eat breakfast at school because Momma walks me there early before work. I've only been back to school for two weeks, but I'm pretty sick of it already. The scrambled eggs at school breakfast come in a big metal tray and are always either too wet or too dry, and they're never hot. The cooks there just don't pay attention like Momma does.

Momma was stirring the eggs this morning when

the phone rang. I wondered who would be calling so early. As I watched Momma's face light up, though, I could tell it was good news. Her eyes brightened and for the first time in a while, she didn't look tired. She looked excited. She looked beautiful.

When she hung up, I absolutely had to ask. "Did you get a new job?"

Momma smiled. "It's just an interview," she replied, "but it sounds good!"

"Who with?" I asked.

"*With whom*," corrected Momma. "It's Children's Hospital."

I was confused. "But you already had an interview with them," I said. The interview was almost a month ago, and Children's had never called back. I remembered because I had been really excited about that hospital. Children's Hospital is very famous and it's less than a mile from home. It is a pretty brick building with different-colored stripes all over it. It doesn't even look like a hospital.

"That's right," said Momma. "That was my first interview. Now they want a second one."

"Why would they interview you twice?" I asked. "Do they think you told a lie in the first one?"

That's the only reason Momma asks me a question twice—when she thinks I'm not telling the truth.

But Momma just grinned. "It means I did a good job the first time around," she explained. "Now the chief nurse wants to meet me. I'm supposed to come by at four this afternoon."

And that's why, at three-thirty, I had to leave Ella upstairs and be watched by Mrs. Okocho.

The front hallway has a creaky, wooden staircase with a fancy carved railing. My sneakers made loud, squeaky thumps on each step as Momma and I walked down.

"Don't fuss, Latasha," Momma ordered.

"I'm not, it's the stairs," I replied.

That was sort of true. I had been stomping a bit, but I wasn't trying to fuss. I was trying to be positive. Being positive meant forgetting about all of the things that I didn't like about Mrs. Okocho, like the smell of her weird cooking and that she is a cheek-pincher. I hoped that by the time I hit the bottom step, I would have stamped out my bad feelings and left them behind.

We reached the front stairwell. I stood in front of Mrs. Okocho's door, looking at its stained glass window.

"Go ahead," Momma said.

I knocked on the door and waited. After a moment, I heard slow, shuffling footsteps and then a shadow appeared behind the glass.

Mrs. Okocho threw open the door and clasped her hands against her chest. "Oh, my blessed word!" she cried in her thick accent. "Look at this young stranger. Little La-la is getting so big!"

My first instinct was to frown. I'd made Momma stop calling me La-la a whole year ago. And clearly I wasn't *that* big or I'd be allowed to stay upstairs like I'd wanted. But I had to make the best of things. So, I stuck out my hand to shake and said, "Thanks for watching me, Mrs. O."

Mrs. Okocho batted my hand aside and "tsk-tsked" through her teeth. "This is a house where we hug," she said, and she pulled me in for a quick squeeze before I could say anything. One of her short, gray dreadlocks almost went right up my nose!

"I must talk with your mama," she said, straightening up. "Go on in, cutie pie!"

The instant I heard *cutie pie,* I knew what was coming. Mrs. Okocho's walk was slow, but her fingers moved like lightning. Just before I could pass, she pinched me hard on my cheek. I hurried on into the apartment.

"I'll be back by six," Momma called after me.

Thank God! I moaned in my head. At least I would be able to eat dinner upstairs. I was barely down the hall and could already smell the strange odor coming from Mrs. Okocho's stove. It smelled kind of...footy.

"Wish me luck, honey!" Momma added.

"Good luck," I said without turning back. I rushed through the kitchen past the wall of neatly arranged pots, pans, and spatulas, past the simmering stew on the stove. Mrs. Okocho always seemed to be making way too much food for one person.

I marched to the far end of the apartment, into a small room that Mrs. Okocho used as her TV room. It was directly below my bedroom. I planned to stay in here, by myself, until it was time to go home. I was glad I'd brought my pocket dictionary and my notebook to keep me busy.

Momma got me the dictionary last Christmas, along with a notebook with an elastic band. Each day, I skim through a few pages of the dictionary. When I see a word I like, I write it down in the notebook. Since Christmas, I've gotten all the way to the letter *N*. I hope to get to *Z* by Christmas this year.

I like my pocket dictionary because it helps me to get a better vocabulary. It is important to have a good vocabulary if you want to be a writer, which is what I want to be after I finish college. I want to write all kinds of songs and poems and books and stories. Also, I like when I am talking to adults and can surprise them with a big word.

I traced down the page with my finger. A nice, long word caught my eye, and I decided to try it out loud. "Ni-tro-gly-cer-in," I said. "Nitroglycerin."

I didn't know how I'd slip the word into a conversation, but its definition was really interesting. Nitroglycerin is a chemical. It is used in dynamite...but also as some kind of medicine!

I wondered if Momma had ever given me dynamite medicine when I was little. It would explain why I get so frustrated sometimes. I was starting to feel embarrassed about stomping off. It was not a mature way to behave. I should have kissed Momma goodbye and wished her luck for real.

The truth was, I really did want her to get this job at Children's. Momma has to take a really long bus ride each way to get to her cleaning job downtown. She could walk to the hospital in fifteen minutes. She would be happier, make more money, and she'd probably get home earlier, too. And I could eat breakfast at home, skip the after-school program, and spend more time with Ella. I glanced up toward my bedroom. I hoped my puppy wasn't too lonely in our quiet apartment.

I heard a cough at the door. Mrs. Okocho was standing there with her hands behind her back.

"Hello, miss," she said.

"Hi," I said.

"Your mama says you don't like for me to call you La-la anymore."

I couldn't believe it. Momma had told her about that? "Well..." I started. "I kind of outgrew it."

"You are a very serious girl now."

I wasn't sure if Mrs. Okocho was making fun of me. "Sometimes," I said carefully.

Mrs. Okocho took her hands out from behind her

back. She was holding a box of craft sticks and some glue.

"Are you too serious for arts and crafts?" she asked.

I smiled. I have to admit, I've always loved the way Mrs. Okocho's accent makes words sound. It turns everyday words like "arts" into something almost musical—*ahhts.*

"Not too serious," I replied, closing up my dictionary and notebook.

Mrs. Okocho pointed to a tall bookcase in the corner, next to the TV. "There are markers on the bottom shelf," she said, and she lumbered off toward the dining room.

I got up to look for Mrs. Okocho's markers. I quietly tried to repeat the last thing she had said. "*Dere ah mah-kahs on de boat-um shelf.*" It didn't sound quite right coming from me—more like a cartoony version of the real thing. But it was close enough to make me giggle.

I knelt down in front of the bookcase. I scanned the dusty bottom shelf and spotted the markers off to one side. They were underneath an orange rubber ball.

I recognized the ball as soon as I moved it. It was Ricky Jenkins's basketball from the summer. It was low on air and had a dent in it. I slid the ball aside, grabbed the markers, and hurried out to the dining room.

Mrs. Okocho had already covered the table with newspapers to protect it from our glue. The chandelier hanging in the middle of the room made the pages look kind of yellow.

"Let us create!" Mrs. Okocho cried.

We worked beside each other for a while. We built, we glued, and we colored with the markers. I had decided to make a house just like this one. I drew little bricks on the walls and then started to work on the porch.

Mrs. Okocho made two karate men and drew a green outfit on one and a black outfit on the other. Then she made them fight. "Wah! Chop!" she yipped.

I rolled my eyes.

"Oh, yes, I forget," she said, putting down her karate men. "We are very serious now."

"Thank you," I said, as I colored the porch brown.

Then Mrs. Okocho did something extremely childish. She stuck her tongue out at me! And held it there. I decided to ignore her. But a whole minute later, she still hadn't moved. In the corner of my eye I saw her, still as a statue—a statue with a pink tongue pointed straight at my head.

I couldn't take the silliness anymore. I just burst out laughing. "Quit it!" I shouted, but I could not be angry one bit.

"You are not so serious," she said, laughing with me.

We kept laughing, until all of a sudden, I heard a terrible rumbling. I let out a small shriek of surprise. The walls rattled and the chandelier shook. The crystals clinked together like wind chimes.

Mrs. Okocho did not seem scared, though. She just let out a growl of frustration.

"What's happening?" I called out over the noise.

"Oh, it is nothing," Mrs. Okocho said sarcastically. "Just a little tornado!"

At first I thought maybe I'd heard the word wrong. Weren't tornados a really big deal? Could they even happen in Pittsburgh?

Then Mrs. Okocho pointed to the ceiling. "A little red tornado," she said with a scowl. And as the rumbling and rattling raced all through the first floor, I finally understood.

Ella had caught another case of the zoomies.

I was so embarrassed that I didn't even know how to apologize. So we just waited out the ruckus—Mrs. Okocho with crossed arms, my head hung in absolute shame. After what felt like half a million years, the storming stopped and there was a final, heavy thump. Ella had fallen asleep.

Mrs. Okocho rubbed the bridge of her nose. "Someone must teach that dog some manners," she said.

I felt like crying. I'd known that Ella was kind of wild. But it was so much worse than I'd thought. My little girl was a natural disaster.

CHAPTER THREE
PUPPY BOOT CAMP

After Ella's tornado act, Mrs. Okocho worked in the kitchen. She swept the floor and stirred her smelly stew. I sat in the dining room, listening. I thought about all the noisy things Ella does each day. Like how her tail beats the side of the stove sometimes when she sits for treats. And how whenever we enter the apartment, Ella jumps up and down to greet us.

Each squeak of the floorboards made me more nervous. What if Mrs. Okocho finally got fed up with Ella's noise? She could lose her temper any day and just say, "No dogs allowed!" I didn't know what we'd do then. She is our landlady, which means she is sort of the boss, even to Momma. Would we have to move? If Ella got us kicked out of our house, Momma would blame me. She'd probably never treat me like a grown-up then.

Luckily, after not too long, Momma came back from her interview at Children's Hospital. It was such a relief to see her—and a bit of a shock, too. Momma opened Mrs. Okocho's door and swooshed in without even knocking! But when I saw her glowing face, I knew why Momma hadn't waited.

"I'm hired!" she shouted.

My mouth opened in a wide smile. But before I could speak, Mrs. Okocho shuffled in from the kitchen. "Sit down, sit down!" she cried. "This is a wonderful!"

When that lady gets excited, grammar just goes out the window. But she had a point. I didn't think I could have said it better. Momma was finally going to be a nursing aide! She would help to care for so many sick kids. I beamed with pride at the thought of it.

Mrs. Okocho pulled out a dining room chair. "Would you like some stew?" she asked. "It is ready to eat."

"Maybe…some other time," Momma said carefully. Then she turned back to me and flashed this funny bug-eyed look. Momma must have liked the smell of Mrs. Okocho's cooking about as much as I did.

I covered my grin with my hand. I liked it when we could share a mother-daughter joke.

Mrs. Okocho came back with a shrug. "Supper will wait, then," she said, and she settled into her chair. "Go on! Tell me all about your new job."

Momma described the things she would be doing at the hospital. She had to keep an eye on things like the patients' temperatures and heartbeats. If anything was wrong, she had to tell the nurse. There were lots of other things, too. I had heard about most of it back when Momma was studying to be a CNA. I didn't pay very close attention, though, to be honest.

But Mrs. Okocho hung on every word. "Ah, such important work!" she marveled. "When do you start?"

Momma leaned forward with her hands on the table. "Two weeks from Monday," she replied. For some reason, Momma looked a little nervous. "The chief nurse wants me to start my shift at eleven a.m."

My eyes grew wide. "That means you can walk me to school!" I cried. "And, we can have a real breakfast together!" So long, soggy eggs in a tray! This was the best news yet, as far as I was concerned.

But Mrs. Okocho had a different reaction. She seemed unusually serious. She put her hand on Momma's and said, "Do not worry. I can help however you need."

"Are you sure it's not too much trouble?" asked Momma.

I was puzzled. Why on earth did Momma want Mrs. Okocho's help making breakfast?

"Momma, you're the scrambled egg master," I told her.

Momma reached over and rubbed my shoulder. I was starting to feel left out and a little annoyed. Had I missed part of the conversation?

"Latasha," Momma said, "Momma's hours are going to be a little different with this new job. I'm going to start at eleven, and I'll work until seven-thirty at night."

That didn't make any sense to me at all! "But…" I stammered. "My after-school program only runs until five, remember?"

"I can drive over and fetch you!" said Mrs. Okocho.

"That would be such a huge help," Momma said. "Thank you."

No thank you! I screamed in my head. I didn't want to ride around in Mrs. Okocho's gross, rusty Oldsmobile. It smells like cigarettes all the time—and she doesn't even smoke!

"Latasha?" asked Momma. "Say 'thank you,' young lady."

Why would Momma take a job that worked so late? Didn't she care if Ella was alone all day? Didn't she care about me? How was I supposed to teach my dog manners if I was never home? A whole bunch of angry feelings swirled around inside of me. I closed my eyes tight and wished them away.

"Latasha Esther Gandy…"

I swallowed hard. I needed to be mature about this. "Thank you, Mrs. Okocho," I said, fighting to keep the shakiness out of my voice.

Right before bed, Ella sat on the floor of our little kitchen. She held her head frozen in place, but her tail jittered behind her, brushing the tile.

This is about as patient as Ella gets.

I was holding a Teddy Snack about a foot above Ella's head. Teddy Snacks are little sweet honey crackers that are shaped like teddy bears. They are Ella's number one favorite treat, which is good because money is always tight in our house and they are a lot cheaper than regular dog treats. She doesn't even mind if they go stale. But I try to remember to close the box up tight anyway.

"Listen up, girl," I said quietly. Momma had told me

to get on my pajamas and I did not want her to hear my talk. "This is serious. I need you to help me. Things are going to change soon. We don't have much time."

She opened her mouth for me to drop the Teddy Snack in. I moved it higher out of reach.

"No treats until you listen," I said. "Good dogs with good manners always listen."

I wasn't sure why I was talking to Ella like she was a person. I knew she couldn't understand all of my words. All I knew for sure was that I had to teach Ella to be good—no, better than good. Perfect.

"We have two weeks to turn you from an April Fool into a model dog," I said. "After that, Momma starts her job. She'll be around less, I'll be around less, and you'll have to be good on your own."

"So…" I went on. I straightened my back and tried to look tough. "Puppy boot camp starts tonight. We'll work hard every day. When we're through, you'll be a master of every command there is. You'll know *sit*, *give paw*, *lie down*, *stay*, *roll over*, and even *take a nap*."

Take a nap means the same thing as *play dead*, only I hate saying *play dead*. It's too creepy and makes me feel nervous.

Ella's tail kept going pitty-pat against the floor. Our talk was going really well, so I decided to give my pup her very first test.

I showed Ella her Teddy Snack treat again and held out my free hand. "Give paw," I said.

Give paw was Ella's best command. She got it right most of the time—actually, all of the time when treats were at stake. She quickly placed her paw in my hand, and I gave her the Teddy Snack.

I fished another treat from the box. Ella offered me her paw again. "No, no paw," I said. "Lie down."

Ella looked at me shyly and raised her paw again. "No paw!" I said firmly. "Lie down. Lie... *down*."

But Ella kept swiping the air with her paw. Why couldn't she ever listen? What was I doing wrong? Finally, I gave in.

"Okay, give paw." I caught her flopping paw, gave it a shake, and fed her the treat. "We'll start again in the morning."

I watched Ella trot off toward my room. "This'll be tough," I sighed.

Tough or not, Ella was my dog and my responsibility. For the next two weeks, I worked with her every single day. I came home from school or errands with Momma, and right away we dove back into training. Except for my homework, I hardly did anything else.

Ella and I always started the same way. I knelt down in our living room with the pup, box of treats at my side. We began with a warm-up of *sit* and *give paw* so that Ella would believe in herself. After ten minutes—and about three times as many Teddy Snacks—we moved on to the command of the day.

I showed Ella every command I wanted her to learn. When I said, "Lie down," I stretched on my belly to teach her how. When I said, "Take a nap," I lay on my side and held perfectly still.

It really confused Ella the first few times I did each command. She just tilted her head and looked at me like I was a total wacko. But after a while, she figured out that she was supposed to copy me. She got a double-treat when she caught on.

Sometimes Momma would come in and interrupt us. Like on Sunday, when I tried teaching Ella *roll over* while wearing my church dress. That was definitely a "Latasha Esther Gandy!" kind of moment.

Most days, though, Momma just let us be until dinnertime. I was glad about that. I really wanted to show her that I could do something important all by myself.

By the end of the first week, Ella had finished off two whole boxes of Teddy Snacks. I didn't want to ask Momma to buy more, so I switched to giving Ella bits of plain white bread instead. I tore the slices up into tiny pieces and just told her they were Teddy Snacks. If my girl noticed the difference, she was a pretty good sport about it.

Before I knew it, it was the last Sunday in September. The next morning, Momma would start her new job and I would go back to Mrs. Okocho's.

On Sundays, Momma and I go to services at the Mount Kimble Baptist Church. Normally, I love church because we have a really great choir. It's like going to a concert every week, and it's free! But today I felt very distracted. All I could think about was Ella.

My girl had done so well during her training. But still, I felt like there was so much left to teach her. The list seemed to get longer every day.

Ella could do the basics, like *lie down* and *stay*. But that hadn't stopped her from putting her paws on the kitchen counter or stealing paper and plastic wrappers from the trash and shredding them up. And it definitely hadn't cured her of her zoomies. That was what worried me the most.

I needed more time. But how could I convince Momma to let me have it? How could I prove that I was big enough to stay with Ella on my own?

After church, Momma and I walked home on Liberty Avenue. That is a street near our neighborhood with lots of little restaurants and shops on it.

As we walked, Momma put her arm around my shoulder. "Tomorrow's a big day," she said. "What do you say we do something special for dinner? We could stop at Pizza Franco."

Then it came to me! I looked at Momma with excitement. "I have a better idea!" I exclaimed. "I'll make dinner for you."

For Momma's special dinner, I had decided to make the tastiest meal I could think of—meatball hoagies! That is my favorite thing to order from Pizza Franco, which is my favorite restaurant.

Here is how you make a meatball hoagie. You spice up some ground meat, mix in breadcrumbs, water, and an egg, and then you shape it all into balls about the size of your fist. You bake the meatballs in the oven, and then you put them on a long loaf of bread with tomato sauce and shredded cheese. Delicious!

We picked up the ingredients from the store on our way home. Then we stopped at a bakery for two small loaves of fresh bread. The loaves each came in their own cute little paper bag, which I liked.

After some more training time with Ella, I got to work on dinner. I started by shredding the block of cheese. That wasn't hard at all. I just rubbed the block on something called a cheese grater and little strings of cheese came out the other side. Ella waited at the edge of the counter for any cheese that fell off, but I only dropped a tiny bit.

Then it was time to make the meatballs. While I read over the recipe, Momma set the oven to heat up. Then I got down to business. Adding the spices was fun. I found them in the cabinet and put them in the bowl with the meat. Then I added the other ingredients. Momma took pictures of each step with our digital camera.

Finally, it was time to mix everything up. But there

was one thing I hadn't counted on—raw meatballs felt *gross*!

"Are you sure you don't want any help?" Momma asked as I mixed the meat up.

"I'm the cook and you're the guest," I replied, my hands deep in the slimy pink slop. I couldn't believe that yummy meatball hoagies looked this awful before they were cooked.

"You don't look like you're having much fun," Momma commented.

"I'm fine!" I snapped.

I was pretty relieved when I finished shaping the meatballs, though. I put them on a tray and washed my hands for about five whole minutes.

"Okay!" I said. "I'll put the meatballs in the oven."

Momma stood up, shaking her head. "Not today," she said. "That's a job for Momma."

I frowned, but it was kind of expected. Momma always said I was not old enough to run the oven myself. I wasn't sure if I agreed, but making dinner had been going too well to argue.

Momma put the meatball tray in the oven. "How long should I set the timer?" she asked.

I glanced at the recipe. "Twenty-five minutes."

Momma set the timer. "I have to do some ironing," she said. "You keep an eye on the clock. When it's almost time, come get me. We'll heat the sauce and cut the bread."

"Can I heat the sauce myself?" I asked.

"If you use the microwave."

I smirked a bit. Things always taste better when you make them on the stove. "I'll wait," I said.

Momma smiled and went toward her room. I heard the jingle of Ella's dog tags behind me. She was still sniffing the floor near the counter where I'd shredded the cheese.

"I think you got it all," I said.

As the timer ticked down, I opened up my pocket dictionary and did some more skimming. I had finished the letter *N* at the after-school program last Thursday. I was now into the letter *O*.

I came across the word *obedient*. It describes someone who listens well. I looked over at Ella, who was lying under the table like a little angel. "You are being very obedient right now!" I told her.

I fetched Momma's camera off the countertop to take a picture, but Ella absolutely would not look at the camera until I held a tiny crust of white bread up as a bribe. So much for *obedient*.

Soon, there were only two minutes left on the meatball timer. "Better go get the boss," I sighed to Ella.

But before I went to fetch Momma, I glanced at the oven one more time. *A real cook would handle the meatballs herself*, I thought.

I'd seen Momma use the oven lots of times. I knew to use oven mitts and how the dials worked to turn the heat off. I knew to put the hot tray on the stovetop and not the countertop. Plus, if I took out the tray and scooped the meatballs onto a plate, I could surprise Momma and save her a little work. I could heat the sauce, melt the cheese, and serve her dinner like she always did for me.

Then I looked at Ella, who was studying my every move from under the table. "You're right," I admitted grumpily. It was best to just listen to Momma and go get her. How could I expect my pup to be obedient if I didn't set a good example first?

I pointed my finger at Ella and said, "You *stay*."

I hurried to Momma's room. She was ironing her work uniform for tomorrow. It was a dark blue shirt and pants that were called *scrubs*. Every CNA at the hospital wore the same color. I was sure that Momma would look the best in hers, though.

"Meatball time!" I announced.

"One sec," she replied. Momma made a few last presses with the iron and unplugged it. We walked toward the kitchen.

"Smells good, sweetie!" Momma said, and I felt all warm inside. I did do a pretty good job when I thought about it.

The timer went off as we passed through the living room. *Oh boy*, I thought. Ella hated the sound of that timer.

But oddly enough, she was quiet. No barking or

running or wild behavior of any kind. I immediately got worried.

I hurried into the kitchen ahead of Momma and saw Ella in the corner. Her head was on the ground and her eyes looked big, wet, and sorry. And then I saw why.

When I spotted the torn paper on the floor, I realized that puppy boot camp had been nothing but a big failure. I didn't even call Ella's full name. I just let out a scream.

In the less-than-one-minute I'd been gone, Ella had eaten both loaves of our hoagie bread whole.

CHAPTER FOUR
FRIENDSHIP

The city of Pittsburgh is not really a city. At least not to me. I think of it as a bunch of small neighborhoods mashed together. I like the neighborhood where I live. Its name is Friendship.

"Look both ways," Momma reminded me.

"I know," I replied.

It was eight thirty on Monday morning. Momma was walking me through Friendship toward my school. I really enjoy walking places with Momma, even though I learned to look both ways when I was four and it's not like I'll suddenly forget or something.

We turned onto the main street of our neighborhood, Friendship Avenue. After a couple of minutes, Momma glanced over at me. "You're being quiet this morning," she observed.

I let out a heavy sigh. "I've got a lot on my mind."

Momma tried to hide a grin. "Oh, yeah?"

"Yeah, I do!" I replied, with a little more attitude than I'd meant to give.

But to my surprise, Momma did not scold me. "Do you want to talk about it?" she asked.

I did want to talk, but I didn't at the same time. I liked

that Momma was taking me seriously for a change, but it was also her first day of work at Children's Hospital and I didn't want to mess up her good mood or make her worry about me.

"I'm okay," I said, and I turned my lips into a smile.

Another few minutes went by and we reached the edge of a small grassy area called Friendship Park. A lot of people in the neighborhood take their dogs there for walks, but Momma always says it is too far for me to take Ella there by myself. I'm only allowed to take her to the end of our block, where Momma can still see me from the house.

In the park, the leaves on the trees were turning from green to red and yellow and brown. Soon, they would litter the ground. People would rake them into piles and bring their kids and their friends and their dogs to play in them. It didn't make sense, but right then, the thought of all that fun made me feel very sad.

Momma said, "You know you can talk to me about anything, don't you?"

I decided to take her up on the offer. "Momma," I said, "does Ella know that she is my friend?"

Momma rubbed my back. "Of course she does, honey," she replied. "She loves you very much."

I wasn't so sure. If Ella was my friend, then why had she wrecked my special dinner last night? Momma had told me that my meatballs were great by themselves, but that wasn't the point. The point was that I had a plan to do something special and perfect, and Ella had ruined it. Didn't she know that best friends don't hurt each other?

Momma and I reached the chain-link fence outside of Cedarville Elementary. Kindergarteners hugged their moms and dads at the curb. Some fourth graders played tag as they hurried toward the front steps.

Momma kissed me goodbye on the cheek. "Good luck today," I told her.

"Thanks, sweetie," she replied. "And don't fret about Ella any more. Just try to have a good day."

"I'll do my best," I replied doubtfully.

"I'm serious, Latasha," Momma said, putting her hands on her hips. "Let's make a deal. When I come home tonight, I promise to bring you a little something that will make you smile. And I want you to have something for me."

Sometimes adults don't make any sense at all! "How can I do that?" I asked. "I don't even have money."

"No, no, I don't want you to buy me anything," she explained. "Just bring me some good news. It can be about something neat that you learned in class, or a game you played on the playground…" Momma raised her eyebrows. "Or even the yummy dinner you'll eat at Mrs. Okocho's tonight."

I stuck my tongue out. "Yeah, right!" I said, laughing. "I'd have a better shot at a yummy dinner if Ella cooked."

Momma chuckled. "Now that's more like my little girl!"

"I'm not a little girl," I reminded her.

"That's even more like her," Momma said, and off she went.

I looked at the large brick building in front of me. *Cedarville Elementary School* was written in big gold letters above the doors. I took a deep breath.

"All right, school," I said, walking toward the doors. "We're going to have an extra fun day, and there's nothing you can do about it!"

It turns out that telling school to be extra fun works about as well as telling Ella to stay. The day was turning out to be normal in just about every way.

During cursive writing practice, I described the way the day felt. "Dreadfully normal," I scrawled, putting a big swoopy curl in the *D.* I love the word *dreadfully*—it's a much more interesting word than *very*, even though they both mean the same thing.

After cursive writing, the day didn't go uphill or down. It stayed absolutely, boringly, flat. It was still early in the school year, so a lot of our lessons were just repeats of things we'd learned last year. By math class, I actually felt kind of bad for our teacher, Mr. Harvey. I liked him a lot, but even the world's greatest teacher couldn't make counting by fives seem exciting.

Then, during recess, it hit me. Unfortunately, *it* wasn't any kind of good news. *It* was a kickball.

Here is what happened. At first, I had wanted to go on the swing set. My plan was to swing higher than any kid ever had before and tell Momma what it was like. But all of the fifth graders were hogging the swing set—and the monkey bars, and the jungle gym—and they wouldn't let anyone else on.

So, I was stuck doing what I normally did. I sat on a bench near the basketball court and did some reading in my pocket dictionary. As everyone else played, I breezed through page after page. I started to get an excited feeling, like I was really close to finding a nifty word that would make Momma smile. But all of a sudden, that feeling was replaced by another feeling.

Whack!

My dictionary flew out of my hands. "Ow!" I cried, grabbing my sore forehead. A red kickball bounced across the ground nearby.

I saw a group of third-grade boys on the ball court. They were all pointing and laughing. All except for

Ricky Jenkins. He was running toward me, his too-large Pittsburgh Steelers jersey clinging to his knees.

"Oh, sorry!" he said. "I didn't mean to get you; it was an accident. We were playing dodgeball. You okay?"

I nodded, fighting back a couple of tears. I was more surprised than hurt.

A kid named Dante Preston shouted out from the court, "It's playtime, not book time, Gandy!"

Dante was a short, wide boy who thought it was cool to call everybody by his or her last name. I scowled at him. He was one of those kids who you just knew was going to grow up to be a bad egg.

"Aw, leave her alone," Ricky told Dante. He picked up my dictionary and handed it to me.

"Why?" Dante scoffed. "She should have been watching!"

"C'mon, man," Ricky said. "She's a girl."

I'm not sure why, but that made me *furious!* I stood up and screeched, "I AM *NOT* A GIRL!"

The boys all laughed as I stalked back toward the school. *I am not a girl?* I thought. That wasn't even true! And the sound… I didn't even know I could make a sound like that. I was so embarrassed.

I stormed back to my classroom. Mr. Harvey was at his desk eating a microwave lunch from a plastic tray. "Latasha!" he exclaimed, quickly wiping his mouth with a napkin.

"You know what, Mr. Harvey?" I asked. "Ella might

be naughty and she might be a bread thief, but at least she's not a *boy*!"

I dropped down at my seat like a lump.

Mr. Harvey came around the front of his desk and leaned back on it. "What happened?" he asked in his deep, kind voice.

I told Mr. Harvey about Ella's episode from the day before. Then I told him about recess. He listened carefully as I spoke, which made me feel better. Even though he'd only been my teacher for a few weeks, he was pretty much the only adult I knew who always took me seriously.

"Well…" Mr. Harvey said, "I think you should give your puppy another chance. She wasn't trying to hurt your feelings. Dogs are different from you and me. They don't think things through."

"Neither do boys," I grumbled.

Mr. Harvey laughed so loud that he had to cover his mouth. "You might be right, Latasha," he said. The class bell rang. It was time for everyone to come back inside.

"But fear not," he added. "We do grow out of that eventually."

Before long, the school day was over. I felt really good about my talk with Mr. Harvey. But that was the only good news I had so far, and that story started with me getting pegged in the head with a kickball. I didn't want to let Momma down. If she was having a bad day, my good news might be the only thing she had to look forward to.

Mrs. Okocho had agreed to pick me up straight after school so that I didn't have to hang out at the after-school program. After the final bell rang, I went outside and waited with the other kids on the front steps.

I kept an eye out for Mrs. Okocho's Oldsmobile.

Oldsmobile is the perfect name for it because it looks like it's older than dirt. Sorry—more *elderly* than dirt.

After a few minutes, I felt a tap on my shoulder. I turned and Ricky Jenkins was standing behind me. He was waiting for his mom to pick him up.

"Hey," he said.

"What do *you* want?" I replied.

"Jeez, don't bite my head off!"

I folded my arms. "Trust me," I stated. "If I was biting your head off, you'd know."

"All right, never mind, then," he huffed, looking like I'd really hurt his feelings.

"Wait," I said. "What's up?"

"I'm just sorry about recess," he told me. "And… I guess I'm sorry I called you a girl."

I let my guard down a little. "I shouldn't have yelled at you," I admitted.

Ricky grinned. "At least you didn't curse me out like your grandma did that time," he said.

I shook my head. "Mrs. Okocho?" I asked. "She's not my grandma. She's our landlady. She's also my… young lady sitter."

Ricky gave me a puzzled look, but then he pointed at something behind me. "Hey, isn't that her?"

I turned and saw Mrs. Okocho's big boat of a car growling down the road. "That's her, all right," I said, thinking of the car's musty, smoky smell.

Ricky held out his hand. "Friends?" he asked.

I shook on it. "Friends."

Ricky smiled. "See ya!" he said, and he ran off.

I couldn't believe it. I'd just made a new friend— and completely by accident!

Mrs. Okocho stopped at the curb with her passenger window rolled down.

"What a cute boy!" she said, much too loudly.

"Oh, gross!" I replied. Boys might not be all bad, but Mrs. Okochos were another story.

I climbed into the car and tried to shut the door, but it wouldn't close all the way.

"No, child," said Mrs. Okocho, waving her hands. "You must slam the door."

I looked at Mrs. Okocho in disbelief. "Really?" First, I had been taught never to slam a door of any kind. Second, I thought that if I slammed this door, the whole car would fall apart in the street.

"Hurry, hurry," she said.

I shrugged and then pulled the door as hard as I could. It shut tight, and the car stayed in one piece.

"And we are off!" she announced. Mrs. Okocho likes to make everything sound like it will be an adventure— even a five-minute car trip.

She also likes to yell at traffic. "Move it, you fool!" she hollered at the car in front of us. "Get off of your phone!"

I usually agreed with how Mrs. Okocho felt about traffic. But Momma is always warning me not to lose my temper, so I kept quiet until we got home to South Graham Street. Besides, I felt so good after forgiving Ricky that I didn't want to spoil it by grumbling.

Mrs. Okocho parked down the street from the

house and we climbed out of the car. "When we get home, your mama said you may check on Ella," she told me.

I didn't need to be told twice. I dashed ahead down our street, pulling out my keys as I ran. I hurried past the flowerbed, onto our porch, and into the house. The steps creaked as I bounded up to our apartment.

Before I could even get my key in the door, I could already hear my girl. Ella's nails were going clickety-clack as she wagged and danced inside our apartment. I smiled so wide it almost hurt my face.

I threw open the door and cried, "Ella!"

Do you know what that crazy pup did in return? She leaped three feet in the air and tried to hug me!

"Whoa!" I said. "You'll knock me down the stairs!" I took a step inside toward safety. Sometimes Ella just has no idea of her own strength.

The pup spun in a circle and leaped up again. "*Down*," I said evenly, kneeling to pet my wild beast. "*Down*."

At that moment, though, I secretly loved her jumping. Anyone who could be that excited to see me absolutely had to be my friend! "I don't know how I could have doubted you," I told Ella as she licked my face. I couldn't wait to share all of my good news with Momma.

CHAPTER FIVE

MR. YUK

But wait was what I had to do. There were four whole hours between the end of school and the end of Momma's shift. Four whole hours of Okocho. Four whole hours apart from Ella.

That was my one big worry. I had taken Ella for a short walk down to the corner and back when I got home. But that was never enough to tire her out. If my lonely pup got the zoomies and made Mrs. Okocho mad, it would just spoil the whole day. The thought of it gave me a nervous feeling in my stomach, like the kind I get before a spelling test.

I sat in the living room, looking out the window. How could I keep Ella out of trouble?

A good friend would take Ella for long walks so that she didn't need the zoomies any more, I thought. But that was out of the question, at least for today.

Then I saw something near our front porch—the flowerbed!

That was the solution. I didn't have to take Ella outside—I had to take Mrs. Okocho outside! She'd never hear Ella going wild out there.

I came into the dining room. Mrs. Okocho was

49

reading the comic strips from the newspaper. "Ah-ha-ha-ha!" she cackled. She said something in Yoruba as she chuckled.

"Mrs. O?" I interrupted.

She peeked over the newspaper, her reading glasses low on her nose. "Are you ready to eat?" she asked. "Your mama left you a sandwich and a salad."

"Not yet," I said, though I was relieved that Momma had thought of me. "Can you take me out front and tell me about your flowers?"

Mrs. Okocho glanced at me suspiciously. "You never had an interest in that before."

"It's for science," I fibbed. We were actually learning about rocks, not plants.

Mrs. Okocho stood up and straightened her dress. "Next time, we do this earlier," she said. "The best sun is gone already."

Mrs. Okocho leaned on my shoulder as we walked down the porch steps. She pointed to her flowers. "Which one would you like to learn about?"

"As many of them as I need to," I said, glancing toward our upstairs window.

"We will begin on the left," Mrs. Okocho declared. "This lovely darling is called… a lily."

For half an hour, I made Mrs. Okocho tell me about each kind of flower she had—where they came from, when they bloomed, how much sun they needed. Some of the flowers had funny names, like kangaroo paw, but mostly I was bored out of my mind! Ella owed me for this.

Really, so did Momma. I was doing everything I could to save this day from disaster. I expected extra good news from her when she got home.

I kept sneaking peeks up toward our window. My ears were tuned in for any sign of the zoomies. But the house was silent. *Leave it to Ella,* I thought. *The only time I ever want her to be bad, she acts like a saint.*

Finally, Mrs. Okocho said, "And that is all of my flowers."

"Wait!" I said. I could barely speak the words as they were so untrue. "I want to know more!"

"Like what?" she asked.

"Like…" I trailed off. I had no idea what to pretend I wanted to learn. "How do you water them?"

"You have seen my watering can, silly girl."

"Sure, but… where did you buy the can?" I asked, racking my brain for any excuse.

"Oh!" cried Mrs. Okocho. "That day was an adventure!"

But as soon as she started to tell her tale, a flash of movement caught my eye. It came from the upstairs window. The curtains were swaying—like a puppy had gotten tangled up in them.

Ella was off to the races! As Mrs. Okocho went on (and on and on) about her watering can, I waited for Ella to run out of steam. The curtain flapped every few seconds as Ella rampaged around the room.

After a couple of minutes, it seemed like things had gone quiet. At least they had inside—Mrs. Okocho was still going on about the day she bought her watering can.

"I was lost in the hardware store for so long that—"

"You know what?" I interrupted. "Let's go inside. I'm getting kind of cold."

Mrs. Okocho smirked. "This is a very boring story, yes?" she said. She looked very disappointed.

"I'm just chilly," I replied. That was only a part-fib. It really had started to cool off.

"Oh, I see!" she realized. "Then we will finish near the heater."

I could hardly wait.

A little before eight o'clock, I heard the front door squeak open. Momma was home at last!

I ran to the hallway and wrapped her in a tight hug. "Yikes!" she said, smiling. "You almost knocked me flat."

Momma thanked Mrs. Okocho for watching me and we went upstairs. Ella did her usual kangaroo-style greeting. She must have been extra excited, because she jumped so hard that she flopped in the air and landed hard on her side.

I dropped to my knees. "Oh, poor baby!" I said, petting her side. But Ella got back up and was fine.

"It looks like you two made up," Momma noted, taking off her coat. She looked so cool in her scrubs, like a nurse on TV.

"That's part of my good news!" I said as I poured

Doggy Chow into Ella's bowl. "But there's lots more."

"Then I'd better sit down," Momma said. She practically fell back into a seat.

I told her the whole story of my day. I told how I'd made friends with Ricky, and how I'd made up with Ella, and even how I'd gotten around the puppy's zoomies.

"Pretty clever," Momma said.

"I know!" I agreed, beaming.

"Still," she remarked, "you shouldn't have strung Mrs. Okocho along like that."

"It was for a good cause?" I replied, uncertain.

Momma rested an elbow on the table. "How would you feel if you were talking and talking and nobody was listening?"

As I heard Ella crunching on her dinner in the background, my first thought was, *I feel that way almost every day!* Instead, I clammed up and just nodded. I didn't want to argue—I wanted to hear Momma's good news for the day.

"What about you?" I asked her, tapping her playfully on the knee. "How was your day?"

"Long!" she said through a yawn.

I stared at her. I knew she was tired, but that was a really lame answer. "That's all you have to say?" I remarked. "Long."

"Yup," she answered. "Things move much faster at the hospital than they do at the hotel. And that's all I have to say about today."

I couldn't believe it! She'd forgotten about our deal! And she'd made the silly thing up. How could she have forgotten about her only daughter?

Momma must have seen the shock on my face. "Hey, I'm just messing around, sweetie," she said quickly. "I didn't forget about our deal. Of course I didn't."

I looked at her with a pout.

"In fact," Momma added, "I got you a little present."

My poutiness dropped away. "Really? Where'd you get it?"

"The hospital gift shop," Momma said, opening her bag.

I didn't even know that Children's Hospital had a gift shop! But of course that made sense. I bet it had all sorts of cool toys. Sick kids could probably use good toys.

But Momma didn't pull a toy from her bag. She pulled out a sheet of glossy paper.

"Check it out," she said, handing it over.

I flipped the sheet over. The other side had a whole bunch of round, bright green stickers on it. Each sticker had a frowny face with its tongue sticking out.

"What's this?" I asked flatly.

"Come on," Momma said. "It's Mr. Yuk!"

"I know it's Mr. Yuk," I said. I wasn't a dummy. I'd learned about Mr. Yuk during preschool at the YMCA. The stickers go on things that are bad for you, like poison and bleach. They mean *stay away!*

"Here's something I'll bet you don't know," Momma said. "Do you know where Mr. Yuk came from?"

Probably the same place where Mrs. Okocho learned to cook, I thought rudely. I knew it was not a mature way to react, but really—what kind of lousy present was this?

"Mr. Yuk was invented at Children's Hospital!" Momma announced.

My eyebrows rose in surprise. "Really?" I asked.

"That's one thing I learned today at work," Momma said. "A doctor thought it up at Children's, and a kid drew the design. I just thought you'd appreciate knowing."

Momma stood up and went to the refrigerator to find a bite to eat.

I looked at my present and smiled. I had to admit, it was kind of neat. Momma worked at the home of Mr. Yuk.

"Back, Ella!" I heard Momma cry. "Get back!"

Ella had pushed past Momma and climbed halfway into the fridge. She was sniffing at a plate of leftover meatballs that were wrapped in foil.

I hurried over and wrestled Ella back by her collar. "Bad puppy," I scolded. I pulled a Mr. Yuk from my sheet and slapped it on the refrigerator handle. "You see that? *No eat.*"

I woke up the next day with Mr. Yuk on my mind. I wondered if I could really use my stickers to train Ella. As I got ready for school, I thought about how to do it.

If I could teach Ella that Mr. Yuk meant *stay away*, then I could put stickers on things I wanted her to leave alone. They could go on important things, like the little box where I keep my earrings. Or on the phone bill—because we still have to pay it even if Ella eats it. I learned about that last March.

Mr. Yuk could be like a guard. I could put a bunch of Mr. Yuks on a string and hang it across the door. Ella would see the string and know to keep out. That would be great, because then Momma wouldn't have to shut the door when she did her ironing.

There was just one problem with my plans. Ella seemed to really like Mr. Yuk. After breakfast I came into my room and found her on the floor with my stickers. She had her front paws on the page and she was licking away at all the Mr. Yuks.

"No," I said, scrambling to take away the sheet. "Mr. Yuk is *yucky. Yuck-eeee.*" I repeated myself a couple of times, trying to make the words sound as gross and nasty as possible. But Ella just grinned her puppy grin like she was very entertained.

I grabbed a book wrapped in brown paper off of my desk. It was my social studies textbook. "Mr. Yuk is *yucky*… like *social studies*."

Social studies is my least favorite subject. I

complained about it all the time, so I hoped Ella would make the connection. I put a Mr. Yuk on the paper book cover.

I pointed to the sticker. "Social studies," I told Ella. "Mr. Yuk. Yucky!"

It was pretty clear to me.

"Time to go, Latasha!" Momma called from the living room. "Take the pup out for a potty."

I hid the stickers as high as I could reach on the bookshelf beside my bed. "We'll talk about this later," I promised Ella, and we hustled off.

All day I thought about how I could get through to my girl. I thought about putting a sticker on the oven. Then I could ring the oven timer a bunch of times, and every time Ella saw Mr. Yuk she'd think of the timer and stay away.

During social studies, Mr. Harvey had us do silent reading in our textbooks. While I was reading, Ricky Jenkins caught a peek of the sticker on my book cover. He nodded his head very strongly and then held up his own book. He stuck his tongue out and frowned to make his face just like Mr. Yuk.

I tried not to laugh out loud. At least I'd gotten through to somebody!

After school, I was so excited to hurry home and try an experiment or two with Mr. Yuk. I'd only have a few minutes before I had to come downstairs, but it would be a start. The hardest choice I had was to pick which idea to test first.

The choice was extra hard because Mrs. Okocho decided to talk my ear off the whole ride home. I wanted to just ignore her and think, but I remembered what Momma had said about really listening, so I tried to pay attention to her every word.

"You will never guess what I see today," Mrs. Okocho said, wide-eyed. "I was this morning driving to the butcher shop."

To de boot-cher shop, I repeated in my head.

"I was on the Friendship Avenue," she continued, "and guess what I see?"

"Traffic?" I replied, realizing she expected an answer.

"A wild turkey!"

I stared at Mrs. Okocho. That was definitely not what I had expected. "A wild turkey," I said.

"A wild turkey!" she repeated. "A wild turkey on the loose, standing right in my lane. I had to stop my car and shoo-shoo it away! Can you believe it?"

I couldn't believe it—probably because she was just making the whole thing up. Everyone knows that turkeys don't live in the city. Sometimes I wonder if any of Mrs. Okocho's "adventures" really happen as she says.

"Hey, Latasha," Mrs. Okocho said. "Why did the turkey cross the road?"

I smirked. "Why?"

She poked me in a ticklish spot on my side. "Because I told it shoo-shoo, turkey!"

Mrs. Okocho laughed and laughed as I squirmed. I decided right then that after my experiment with Ella, I would hide in the TV room for the rest of the day and not say another word to her.

I dashed out of the car the second we parked. I hurried upstairs. With each step, I got less frustrated and more excited. I couldn't wait to greet my jumping little pup.

Except that when I opened the door, there was no jumping pup.

I entered the living room. "Ella?" I called out. On the floor, I saw shreds of glossy paper.

I ran into my room. It was a wreck! My bed sheets were bunched up like they'd been walked on and books from my bookshelf littered the floor.

I spotted more glossy shreds all over the room. One of the shreds had a Mr. Yuk sticker on it. At that moment I realized it—Ella had eaten the rest of them.

I knelt down to save my one last Mr. Yuk. "Ella," I uttered. The puppy was hiding under my bed. Her whole body had disappeared except for her tail, which was wagging out in the open.

"Ella," I said calmly. I really felt like yelling, but I

knew that if I did, I'd never get her out. I hid the last Mr. Yuk in my pocket. "Ella, come here."

I saw the tail disappear under the bed, and then Ella poked her head out. When I saw her face, it got very hard to stay mad. Half of a Mr. Yuk was stuck to the edge of her lip. She was trying to lick it away, but with no luck.

"My bad little girl," I said with a sigh.

I plucked the half-sticker off her lip and looked at it in frustration. All of my training plans were ruined! But then, a nervous feeling swept over me. Ella had eaten a whole lot of those stickers. Could all that sticky stuff hurt her tummy? What if they made a sticky ball and got stuck inside her?

"Are you okay, puppy?" I asked.

I couldn't tell just by looking at Ella, but I knew someone who could help. I looked at the back of Ella's dog tag, ran to the phone, and dialed.

After one ring, someone picked up. "Vanderstam Veterinary, how can I help you?" It was Miss Simon. She was a helper who answered the phone at our vet's clinic.

"Can I please speak with Dr. Vanderstam?" I said, trying to sound relaxed. Ella had followed me to the phone and I did not want to worry her.

"Is this Latasha?" asked Miss Simon.

I answered that it was. I was a bit embarrassed that Miss Simon could recognize my voice—I guess I call the clinic a lot.

"Maybe I can help you," Miss Simon offered. "What's the matter?"

I raced through the whole story without even stopping for breath. "Is she going to be hurt?" I asked, rubbing Ella's head behind her ear.

"Don't worry," said Miss Simon. "Ella will be okay."

I breathed out and let my shoulders loosen up. Miss Simon was a good person to talk to. Her voice always sounded like she was smiling.

"So stickers won't hurt her?" I asked.

"Well," Miss Simon replied, "don't start feeding them to her every day."

"I know," I said with a grin.

"Is there anything else I can help with?" she asked.

I noticed that Ella had walked away. She was nosing through the paper scraps on the living room floor.

"Why is she so bad all the time?" I asked, annoyed all over again. "She eats things that aren't food, she runs all over the place…."

The last part was hard to even say out loud. "I feel like I'm a really lousy dog mom," I admitted.

"I'll tell you a secret, Latasha," said Miss Simon. "Do you know how you can make a dog behave all of the time?"

"How?" I asked, nearly jumping through the phone.

"You can't," she replied.

I huffed dramatically.

"But do you know how you can make a dog behave most of the time?" asked Miss Simon. "You get it good and tired! A tired puppy is a good puppy."

I felt like I'd gotten nowhere. I knew I needed to get Ella more exercise, but I didn't know how. I sat downstairs and thought it over.

I guessed that I could try doing our normal short walk a bunch of times in a row. But that seemed like it would just be boring. I needed to take Ella someplace fun and far from the house—like Friendship Park. To do that, though, I'd have to have someone go with me.

I heard Mrs. Okocho clang a pot onto the stove.

Could I ask her to take us? Momma would have to agree to that.

Mrs. Okocho poked her head in. "Care for a snack?" she asked. "I am making oxtail pepper soup!"

I wrinkled my nose. "No, thanks," I said. I refused to eat anything with *tail* in the name. Maybe I wouldn't ask Mrs. Okocho after all. She walked slowly anyway, and she would probably just take up the time with more of her silly stories and jokes. Or she'd want to have a weird, smelly oxtail soup picnic.

Then, I saw the answer. It was staring at me, tucked on the bottom bookshelf—Ricky Jenkins's basketball.

I could not believe I hadn't thought of it before! I didn't need help from Mrs. Okocho or Mr. Yuk. I needed help from Ricky. We could walk Ella to Friendship Park together. We could rake up leaf piles and let Ella jump through them, and then run the puppy up and down the grass until she was so tired that we had to carry her home.

I was pretty sure that Ricky would go along with my idea. He loved doing stuff outside. I just hoped that Momma would trust us enough to go along, too.

CHAPTER SIX

THE TURKEY HUNT

It took me all night to find the nerve to talk to Momma. I was kind of afraid to ask about taking Ella for walks. If Momma said no, I didn't really have any other plans. But the next morning, as we passed Friendship Park on the way to school, I decided to be brave.

I thought it would be best to start slowly. "Momma…" I eased in. "If I went with a friend, could I come here to the park after school?"

"Who's this friend?" she asked.

I reminded Momma about how I'd made friends with Ricky Jenkins from across the street.

"Well…" she said, thinking it over.

"I'll tell Mrs. Okocho exactly when I'll be back, and I'll come home not a minute later," I promised. "And if I am late, she can tell you, and you can ground me for as long as you'd like."

Momma laughed. "Thank you for the permission!"

"So, am I allowed?" I asked.

Momma looked down at me. "You can go to the park with Ricky," she said. "But you have to stick together the whole time. If he decides he doesn't want to go, then you have to stay home."

"Of course!" I said. I hoped that Momma didn't really think I needed to be told that.

We walked a little farther before I got to my real point. I put my hands in my coat pockets. My fingers found my one last Mr. Yuk sticker. I'd put it in there for luck. "There's one more thing I wanted to ask," I said.

"You want to bring Ella," Momma predicted.

How did she always do that? There just was no being sneaky with her.

"That *would* be a nice thing to do," I said, as if I'd just thought of it.

"I had a feeling," she said. "The answer is yes."

I hugged Momma's arm hard. "Thank you!" I exclaimed into her sleeve.

"Just remember that Ella can be a real handful," Momma said. "If she gets too riled up, you have to take her right home."

"I will," I agreed.

Now I just had to get Ricky on my side. I wanted to talk to him before school started, but Ricky got to homeroom just as the bell rang, so I had to wait until recess.

I walked over to the grassy patch where Ricky was tossing a Frisbee with Dante and his friends.

"Hey, Ricky," I said.

"Look, Jenkins," said Dante, out of breath from running. "It's your girlfriend!"

"You're hilarious," I said, giving him my best death stare. I didn't know why Ricky hung out with that kid.

Ricky turned with the Frisbee. "Hey, Dante," he said with a devilish grin. He hurled the disc all the way across the grass to the fence. "Go get it!"

Dante grumbled and ran off, huffing and puffing. Ricky and I walked to the benches and I explained how I needed a partner to take Ella to the park.

"So I can count you in, right?" I asked.

Ricky shrugged. "I don't know."

I gaped at him. "What do you mean you don't know?"

"Going dog walking sounds kind of boring," he answered.

Then you haven't met Ella, I thought.

"Maybe some other day," Ricky said, and he stood up from the bench.

My plan was crumbling before my eyes. "Wait, wait," I said in a panic. "I haven't even told you about the really cool part yet!"

Ricky stopped to listen. "What cool part?"

I blinked. I didn't have an answer. Walking Ella kind of was the really cool part. "There's…" I said, fumbling for the words. "There's this…"

"You're a little odd sometimes," Ricky said, and he turned to leave again.

"There's a wild turkey in Friendship Park!"

Ricky turned back in total surprise. "A turkey?"

I hadn't meant to lie. It had just sort of spilled out. But there was no turning back now. "There's a turkey that's living near the park," I said. "If we take Ella out there, maybe she can help us find it."

Ricky broke out into a grin. "You're yanking my chain," he said.

"Mrs. Okocho saw it yesterday," I insisted. "I guess it got loose from a farm and wandered into town. Wouldn't it be cool to see a wild turkey?"

After a few seconds, Ricky said, "Four o'clock today. We'll meet up at my house."

"Awesome!" I said.

"You really think your dog can help us find it?" asked Ricky.

"Sure," I replied with a shrug. "Ella's part hunting

dog."

Well, that last part *could* have been true.

At first I was proud of my quick thinking. But as the day went on, I began to feel guilty for being dishonest. It was important to get Ella out for a walk—no, it was *dreadfully* important. But telling fibs is wrong and definitely not a mature thing to do. It can be really hard to make the right choice sometimes!

Once I got home, I decided that I would tell Ricky the truth. He would be disappointed about the turkey. But I hoped that once he met my cute little mutt, he'd like her so much that he'd come along for her walk anyway.

Just before four o'clock, I went upstairs, put my jumping pup on her leash, and took her down the steps. As always, Ella tried to lead me directly into Mrs. Okocho's flowerbed. "*No*," I said. She gave a daisy one quick lick, and then she actually listened and trotted onto the grass. We were off to a great start!

We walked across the street and I rang Ricky's doorbell. Ricky opened the door right away. He had a bulge in the pocket of his hooded sweatshirt. He swung his head back and yelled, "I'm going, Mom, be back soon!"

Ricky stepped out and closed the door. "Hi there!"

he said to Ella. She began to wag her tail like mad—she was swinging so hard that she kept hitting herself in the face with it! It didn't stop her, though. She just kept wagging and flinching at the smack of her tail.

I tried to block the tail with my arm. "Settle down, you'll put your eye out!" I said. That's what Momma always tells Ella when her bendy body gets out of control.

Ricky just laughed. "She's funny," he said as he reached out to her. Her tail settled a little as she happily licked his hand.

I could tell that Ella and Ricky would make good friends. It seemed like the right time to admit my little turkey trick. "Ricky—"

"Come check this out," he cut in. Ricky bounded down the steps and started walking down the sidewalk. Ella yanked me along to follow him.

When we were a few houses down, Ricky reached into his sweatshirt's pocket. Glancing back toward his house, he slyly pulled a tall, round cardboard container out. I looked at the label.

"Breadcrumbs?" I asked.

"Yeah, for the turkey!" he replied. "I swiped them from my mom's pantry. We can use them as bait in the park. I was thinking that turkeys probably love breadcrumbs. Because breadcrumbs are how you make stuffing, and that's what you always have with turkey at Thanksgiving. What do you think?"

Ricky looked at me with bright, excited eyes. I could tell that he had been thinking about our turkey hunt all afternoon. He was so pumped up that I didn't have the heart to be honest.

"It sounds like a plan to me," I said.

We walked Ella down to the corner. I smiled to myself as we passed Coral Street. It was the first time I'd left my block without an adult at my side.

Ricky, Ella, and I slowly made our way toward Friendship Park. It was slow because Ella completely refused to go anywhere in a straight line. She preferred to move in jerks and jumps. She would pull ahead faster than I wanted to go, and then suddenly stop, rush off to the side, or loop around and wrap me up in her blue leash.

Every mailbox and tree and sign post was like some fascinating mystery to her. She had to dart over and give each one a good, long sniff.

I wish I'd brought some Teddy Snacks, I thought grouchily. I'd forgotten how stubborn Ella could be on a walk. On any other long walk, Momma had always been there to sternly say *No!* and keep her in check.

"Come on, girl," I said as she pressed her nose against her fifteenth telephone pole. I was starting to run out of patience. If she kept taking a rest every ten feet, I'd never get her zoomies out.

Ricky, on the other hand, didn't mind Ella's curiosity one bit. "I'll bet she smells the turkey," he kept saying.

I shrugged with a smile, but on the inside my stomach was tying itself into knots. That poor kid was going to really hate me when he found out the truth.

After ages and ages, we made it to the edge of the park. It looked just as perfect as I'd hoped. An elderly man with a plaid hat was reading the newspaper on a bench. Some joggers were running on the sidewalk. One jogger had a golden retriever with him. It was following nicely behind.

I leaned down by Ella's ear. "See that?" I whispered. "That is how a good dog walks." Ella panted lightly as I petted her head.

Of course, the calm moment didn't last. Ricky pulled open his can of breadcrumbs and shouted, "Come on out, turkey!" He grabbed a fistful of breadcrumbs and hurled them ahead.

The crumbs pelted the grass and Ella shot off so hard that she nearly pulled me off my feet. I thought she was going to tear my arm off!

"Ella Fitzgerald Gandy!" I hollered. The golden retriever barked as if to egg Ella on—like she really needed the encouragement! I hurried to keep up with Ella as she fought her way to the food on the ground. She hungrily lapped it up, taking some blades of grass along for the ride.

Ricky ran up behind me. "Man, bad idea," he said.

"You think?" I asked, rubbing my shoulder over my coat.

I noticed that the elderly man had stopped really reading his newspaper and was only pretending to read. He was actually watching Ella. I wanted to yell, *I'd like to see you do better!* But I decided to be the adult one and ignore him.

"I'll hold off on the breadcrumbs from now on," Ricky said, hiding the can back in his sweatshirt. "See, Ella? All gone."

Holding the leash with my other arm, I let Ella lead us around the park. If I hadn't known better, I might have really believed she was tracking our friend the wild turkey. She circled each tree and raced in zigzags through the grass.

Ricky stayed with Ella at every turn, asking her questions about the hunt. "What is it, girl? Do you think it went in the bush? This wild turkey is a sneaky fellow, isn't he?"

"She's not Lassie, you know," I finally snapped.

"I know that," Ricky retorted. "It's called having fun. You ought to try it sometime, grumpy-grump."

I didn't say anything back. I was actually really glad that Ella was having so much fun. She deserved to have a great time like this every single day. It was just that every time Ricky opened his mouth about the turkey, it made me feel like a real jerk for tricking him.

After half an hour, Ella's pace slowed to a trot. We'd finally tired her out. There was no way she'd annoy Mrs. Okocho tonight.

One of the park benches was open, so Ricky and I took a seat. Ella dropped down in the grass at our feet. "I think she's done for the day," Ricky said.

I nodded in satisfied agreement.

"You want to come looking again tomorrow?" he asked. "I have a net I could maybe bring. I should have brought it today. It's really for catching butterflies, but it's pretty big."

"Ricky…" I said, my voice a little shaky. I reached in my pocket and touched the glossy backing of my lucky

Mr. Yuk. "I have to tell you something really important."

"Let me guess," he said. "You made this whole wild turkey thing up."

I stared at him.

"Yeah, I figured that out a while ago," he added as if it was no big deal at all.

"When did you figure it out?" I asked, astonished.

"At school," he replied. "The whole story was kind of hard to believe anyway. But you also started acting a little nervous after lunch. Like you were afraid of being caught at something."

I could not believe that I'd worried so much over nothing. It was actually a little bit frustrating that Ricky was so calm. "Then why'd you go along with it?" I demanded.

"I thought it would be fun to pretend we were turkey hunters," he said with a shrug. "Ella sure liked it."

Ella was resting her head on my sneaker. She looked at me and smiled with her tongue flopped out almost to the ground. It made me feel like the most loved girl in all of Pittsburgh.

"So," Ricky said, "should I bring the net tomorrow or not?"

CHAPTER SEVEN

THE QUEEN OF BOOK MOUNTAIN

On Friday afternoon, Mr. Harvey made a huge announcement.

"The weekend's almost here, ladies and astronauts," he said. Mr. Harvey always has the funniest sayings. "Tomorrow is the first day of October. Can anyone tell me what we celebrate in October?"

A girl in the front row named Darla Robinson raised her hand immediately. She always tries to be the first to answer any of Mr. Harvey's questions. "Halloween," she declared.

"That is correct, Darla," Mr. Harvey replied, "but it's not quite the answer I was looking for. What I meant to ask is this: What do we celebrate during the whole month of October?"

Then I realized—I knew this! "October is National Book Month!" I called out.

I learned about National Book Month back in kindergarten when I got the chicken pox in October and had to miss a whole week of school. Momma got me a stack of books to read from the library and a special National Book Month bookmark.

Mr. Harvey smiled and said, "That's right, Latasha!" Then he added, "Even if you didn't raise your hand before speaking."

I smirked, but I guess he sort of had to mention it.

"To celebrate National Book Month," Mr. Harvey went on, "Cedarville Elementary School is holding a special reading contest. Its name is Book Mountain!"

A few of my classmates whispered to each other. "What do we have to do?" asked a girl from behind me.

"It's very simple," Mr. Harvey replied. "All each of you has to do is read as many books as you can during the month of October. On November first, each teacher will tally up how many books his or her class has read. And the class with the highest count gets to have their very own pizza party!"

Everyone ooh-ed and whooped and cheered. I hoped that we could get the pizzas from Pizza Franco, but I thought it would be silly to ask about it right then.

Dante Preston raised his hand and waved it. "Can we get mushroom and sausage pizza?" he begged.

"Let's not get ahead of ourselves," Mr. Harvey replied. I held back a grin. "We have a lot of reading to do before we pick out our toppings. And a lot of writing, too."

Ricky raised his hand. "I thought this was just a reading contest," he said.

"Ah, yes!" our teacher said, as if he'd forgotten something. "Well, this is a reading contest. But we have to make sure that the students have actually done all of the reading they say they have. I don't believe that any of *you* would try to trick me, of course. But between you and me, I hear those first graders can be awfully sneaky."

I giggled with some of the other kids in my row. "So," Mr. Harvey continued, "for each book you read, you have to write a short summary for me to check."

Some of the giggles and cheers were replaced by groans. But I just smiled. I was already making a list of all the books I could read.

After school, Ricky came by the house to help me walk Ella. The puppy pulled me down the porch steps to say hello, her whippy tail clipping my calves.

"No net today?" I asked Ricky.

"I don't really feel like playing turkey hunter," he said. "You think Ella will mind?"

"She'll get by," I replied. I was secretly very relieved. I didn't think I could take a third day in a row of pretend hunting. Yesterday, Ricky had actually brought his big net to the park. He and Ella had a great time, but I thought we looked awfully silly lugging it around.

We began our stroll. Ella was her usual self, sniffing every object we passed as if she'd never ever been on a walk before. But Ricky did not seem like his usual self at all. He walked glumly along a few steps behind, quiet as a mouse.

"What's the matter?" I asked him.

"Can you believe we have to do all that writing for Book Mountain?" he asked with a frown.

I shrugged. To tell the truth, the writing part was actually the thing about Book Mountain that got me most excited. I was looking forward to going through my notebook full of dictionary words and using as many of them as I could. Mr. Harvey would be very impressed with my reports.

But I didn't say any of that. I just said, "It probably won't be so bad."

"Easy for you to say," Ricky scoffed. "You're really smart."

I felt my cheeks get warm. But then I realized what Ricky really meant. "Hey, you're smart, too!" I replied.

Ricky looked at me doubtfully. "Can I tell you something?" he asked.

I started to say, "Definitely!" But at that instant, Ella tried to run ahead across the street, so I had to settle for, "Bad dog, stay!"

Once Ella relaxed, I gave Ricky the nod to go ahead.

"I'm a really bad reader," Ricky said as we crossed the street.

"That's not true," I replied. I wasn't just being nice, either. At the beginning of the year we each had to give a report on "How I Spent My Summer Vacation." Ricky read a story about how he and his dad went to see the Pittsburgh Steelers training camp, and he didn't even mess up once.

"Well, I guess I'm not a bad reader," he said. "But I'm bad at describing the things I read. I can never pick out what's important to a story and what's not. It feels like it takes me almost as long to write a book report as it does to read the book."

"You know what helps me write a book report?" I asked. "I like to imagine that I'm telling the story to my mom."

That weekend, though, Momma did not seem very interested in anything I had to say. She was tired from the past week and worried about everything she had to do before the next one began.

"I have bills to write out, we have to get to the grocery store and shop for the week, and let's not forget the laundry—"

"—Ella needs a refill on her Doggy Chow," I added helpfully. *And maybe a new chew bone*, I added in my head. Ella had been so good since Ricky and I had started walking her. She hadn't had her zoomies one time, and she slept all night on the end of my bed instead of roaming around and smooshing my ankles in the middle of the night. If that wasn't worth a little present, I didn't know what was!

"And a trip to Pet Planet, too," she said with a sigh. "Sweetie, I don't think we have time for the library today."

"It's for school!" I protested. Momma had always made time for the library before.

"Don't be difficult, Latasha," she said. "The library won't float away before tomorrow."

That was true, but waiting would really wreck my schedule for Book Mountain. I wanted my class to win, and I wanted to be the number one reason we did. My plan was to read a book a day on the weekends and make it through one more book during each school week. That would give me an even dozen, a number not even Darla Robinson could top. But I had to begin today!

My October was off to a lousy start. I fell back heavily onto my bed. Ella hopped up near my waist and settled across my ribs like she was giving me a hug. She was a heavy girl, but it felt kind of nice anyway.

A sound came up from below my bed. It came from the heating vent—it was a high-pitched laugh, like a witch's cackle. I realized that it belonged to Mrs. Okocho. She was downstairs in her TV room, watching her Saturday morning cartoons without a care in the world.

"And here we arrive!" cried Mrs. Okocho, parking her car.

Momma was too busy, but Mrs. Okocho was more than happy to give me a ride to the Carnegie Library. It is a couple miles from home, in a neighborhood called Oakland.

As we approached the children's section, I was nervous that Mrs. Okocho would hang around and do something silly or embarrassing. But thankfully, she had a book of her own to find. "You stay here," she said. "I will return soon."

The children's section was decorated all over with signs for National Book Month, as well as with hanging cutouts of ghosts and bats for Halloween. The librarian offered me a list of books for third and fourth graders from her desk, but I was happier to just search on my own. I knew what I wanted—short books, but ones that would be a challenge with words that I would have to look up.

I searched up and down the aisles. Hunting for books was so much more fun than hunting for made-up turkeys! I found a fun-looking book about a talking fox and an old one about a family living in the woods.

I grabbed a picture book from the biography shelf. It was not quite what I'd planned on getting, but I just couldn't pass it up. It was about my favorite singer, Ella Fitzgerald! I decided to read it to my puppy so that she would know where her name came from.

To balance things out, I also picked an extra tough book—an old ghost story called *The Legend of Sleepy Hollow*. I didn't know what to expect, but it seemed like the right kind of book for October. Plus, the print was very small, like a book for grown-ups. I decided to read that one first.

Soon, I'd collected my dozen books for the month. As I made my way back to the desks and computers, I held my picks up high on my chest. I felt much more mature having a stack of books that almost touched my chin. Now I just had to find Mrs. Okocho.

"Boo!" a voice hissed from behind me. I jumped halfway to the ceiling and my books crashed to the floor.

I whirled around. I didn't have to find Mrs. Okocho after all. She'd found me. I glared at her and whispered, "Shh!" Even the preschoolers were starting to stare.

"Happy Halloween," she whispered back, a month too early.

The next couple of weeks flew by. Momma went back to work on Monday, and I went back to school. Day after day, we all turned in our book reports. Mr. Harvey always returned them the very next morning. He kept a tally on the chalkboard of our progress. On some days, he gave us reminders that we were supposed to stick to books on our reading level.

"*Green Eggs and Ham* is a little young for third grade, Dante," I heard him say.

"But it was written by a doctor!" Dante protested.

Mostly, though, Mr. Harvey had only good things to say. He left us lots of nice notes on our papers, like *What an interesting report!* On my summary of *The Legend of Sleepy Hollow,* he wrote *Stellar!* That means *awesome*—I think Mr. Harvey picked the word just so I'd have to look it up.

After school each day, Ricky and I took Ella to the park. At the park, it was Ella time. We played and ran and took blurry pictures of her that I saved on our computer at home. But on the way there and back, we talked about the books we were reading. I had Ricky describe the plot of his latest book, hoping that it would help him to write his book report.

I think it did help, because on Tuesday of the second week, Ricky got his first book report back and it said, *Nicely done!* Ricky was not impressed, though. "I don't think Mr. Harvey actually reads them," he said with a shrug.

"He absolutely does!" I replied.

Ricky gave me a light bump with his elbow. "How would he have time for mine?" he asked. "You've probably turned in like a thousand of them by now."

I hoped he couldn't see me blushing.

Other times, when Ricky wasn't in the mood to talk about Book Mountain, we just asked each other questions. Ella always trotted between us, turning her head to watch each of us talk like it was a game of ping-pong. By the middle of the month, Ricky pretty much knew more about me than anyone, except Momma.

"It's cool that your mom's a nurse," Ricky told me.

"Nursing aide," I corrected.

"I'll bet she has a ton of cool stories, though," he said.

I shook my head. "She's just worn out when she gets home," I replied. I almost didn't even add the worst part. "Sometimes… sometimes she doesn't even ask me how my day was."

I was starting to wonder if Momma's new job was really better than working as a cleaning lady.

During the third week, I read a book about two sisters and their mother. In the book, the older sister didn't call her mother *Momma*. She called her *Mother*. I liked the way it sounded when I read it to myself, so on Wednesday I decided to try it out.

When Momma got home, I hurried to the front hallway to hug her. "Welcome home, Mother!" I said.

Momma gave me a weary smile and rubbed my back. She looked even more tired than usual, like she'd been on her feet for days instead of hours.

We went upstairs to greet Ella. She leaped and licked hello, but Momma just brushed past her and set her purse down on the kitchen counter.

I got the pup's dinner ready. "Ella was so good on her walk today, Mother," I said.

"Was she?" Momma commented as she shuffled containers aside in the fridge.

I wasn't sure what I had wanted out of this little test, but I knew I wasn't getting it. "All right, *Mother*," I said, "I'm going to go read some more."

Momma turned with a carton of skim milk in her hand. "What?" she asked.

"I'm going to go read my book some more," I repeated, frowning. "It's about these girls and their *mother*."

"Oh, okay," Momma said. "You read. I'll take Ella out for her potty tonight."

She said it like it was some big important favor.

I told Ricky about my failed *Mother* experiment the next afternoon. "Can you believe it?" I asked. "She didn't even notice!"

"Maybe she just had an extra tough day," Ricky guessed. "It probably gets pretty sad being around sick kids all the time."

We walked on. For a while, the only sounds were the cars passing by and Ella's jingling collar as she trotted between us. I wished I could be more like Ella sometimes—then I wouldn't notice that Momma spent more time thinking about the kids at her work than she did about me.

"Hey, Latasha," Ricky finally said. "When we get back, can I borrow one of your old reports?"

I was glad that Ricky had changed the subject. "I guess so," I answered. "Why?"

"I just want to see how you write your summaries," he said. "I was thinking that if I had a good example to go from, maybe it'd help me write better ones myself."

Ricky's habit of making me blush had actually become a bit of a nuisance.

School the next day was pretty normal. We had silent reading and math and social studies, and in the afternoon we had our Friday art class with Mrs. Yarding. We painted monster masks, which was a lot of fun.

The day breezed by until the final bell rang. We all packed up our backpacks and began to leave. "Latasha, Ricky," Mr. Harvey called out. "Stick around a minute."

I glanced at Ricky and he shrugged. We stayed inside and took a seat in the front row, across from Mr. Harvey's desk.

"You guys don't have to catch the bus, right?" asked Mr. Harvey.

We both shook our heads.

"Good, because we need to talk," he said. He shifted uncomfortably in his chair.

"What's the matter?" I asked.

"I found out something very disappointing today,"

he replied. "I really couldn't believe it."

Ricky's expression became disturbed. "Mr. Harvey—"

"I can't believe you two thought I wouldn't notice," our teacher interrupted.

"Us two?" I said hurriedly. "I didn't do anything!"

Mr. Harvey gave me a look of such disappointment that I thought I would melt into my chair. He laid a sheet of paper down on my desk. It was a book report. The title was: *The Legend of Sleepy Hollow*… by Ricky Jenkins.

I looked over at Ricky in shock. He gave me the same shy glance that Ella does when she's been bad.

"Do you think I don't actually read these?" Mr. Harvey demanded.

"Yeah, kind of," Ricky replied. I closed my eyes and shook my head at his answer.

"Well, I do," Mr. Harvey responded sharply. I'd never seen him start to lose his cool before. I didn't speak. I was worried that if I opened my mouth, I might throw up.

Mr. Harvey stood up from his desk. "When you tried to cheat, you didn't just let yourselves down. You let the whole classroom down." He looked right at me. "You should have known better."

Throw up or not, I had to say something. "Mr. Harvey, I didn't know anything—"

"Save it, Latasha," he replied with a wave of his

hand, like he was swatting my words away. "I'm going to have to disqualify you from Book Mountain. The both of you."

I ran out the front doors of the school. Mrs. Okocho's car, late as always, was nowhere to be seen. I flexed the muscles in my face and ordered myself not to cry.

Ricky rushed out behind me. "Latasha," he called after me.

"Go away," I commanded.

"I'm really sorry, okay?" he said. "I didn't mean to get you in trouble."

"I tried to help you!" I said in a quavering voice.

"I'll talk to Mr. Harvey first thing Monday and fix things. I'll tell him the truth, that I tricked you."

"Just great!" I exclaimed. "So I'm not a cheater—I'm just too dumb to realize that you are."

"I didn't think," Ricky admitted. "I'm the dummy here. You shouldn't get punished. I just…"

Ricky kept talking, but the sorrier he acted, the madder it made me. Thankfully, Mrs. Okocho's car pulled into view around the corner. It couldn't get here fast enough.

"At least we didn't get detention, right?" Ricky said hopefully.

That was the last straw. He didn't understand what had happened, not one bit. I wanted to scream in his face. But in all of my reading, in books or my pocket dictionary, I hadn't found any words terrible enough to call him. I remembered all the things we'd talked about, and how I'd trusted him, and how it was all ruined. I felt the tears welling up. I jammed my hands in my coat pockets and squeezed.

Then I found it. I'd forgotten it was in there.

As Mrs. Okocho's Oldsmobile reached the yellow curb, I pulled a piece of glossy paper from my pocket. I peeled off my last Mr. Yuk sticker and slapped it right on Ricky's chest. Then I turned my back on him for good.

CHAPTER EIGHT
THE LONGEST NIGHT

Ella greeted me as if nothing had happened. She wiggled and whacked me with her tail as I knelt down to pet her. She licked at my face—she probably smelled the salt from the tear or two that I couldn't hold back.

I went to the counter and fed Ella a treat. "You might be sneaky sometimes," I told her as I gave her a hug, "but you're not a cheater."

I still couldn't believe that Ricky would try to cheat off my work. And he'd lied to me about it, too. It was making me wonder what else Ricky had lied about. Was he pretending to be my friend the whole time? Were he and Dante and the others laughing at me right now?

And Mr. Harvey thought I was a liar and a cheater, just like Ricky. I was already thinking up ways I could play sick on Monday so that I wouldn't have to face him again. But if I played sick, then I really would be a liar. There was no way to escape. I felt like a foolish little kid.

I had to push the bad thoughts out of my head. I grabbed Ella's leash to take her out. "Go potty?" I asked.

Ella's ears pinned back and she wiggled in excitement. But when I brought the leash close, she ran out of the kitchen!

I sighed and followed her into the living room. Ella was running in circles near the window. When she reached the window, she swiped the curtains aside with her nose and reached up onto the sill to look out.

I laughed at the silly pup and came over to put the leash on her. But when I moved the curtains, I saw what Ella was looking at. The view from that window was of Ricky's house.

"No, no, no!" I shouted. Ella dropped off the sill and lay down on her belly. I was scaring her.

I slumped down next to her. "I'm sorry, Ella," I said, stroking the back of her neck. "It's just you and me again."

I didn't need Ricky. I didn't need Mr. Harvey or Momma either. I just needed my sweet little Ella. And as I gripped her leash, I knew exactly what I had to do to feel better.

"I'm taking Ella out!" I shouted from the front hallway.

"I can tell!" said Mrs. Okocho from inside. I guessed it was pretty obvious. Ella's crazy tail was drumming the walls and her nails clacked on the steps as she danced at the end of her leash.

"We'll be back in an hour," I called out.

"Say hi to Ricky for me!" Mrs. Okocho replied.

Fat chance, I thought.

When we got out the door, Ella pulled me down the steps and toward the curb. She tried to cross the street toward Ricky's, but I gave the leash a firm jerk. "Not anymore," I reminded her.

We walked by ourselves down South Graham Street. Ella tried to do her normal stop-and-sniff routine, but I was not in the mood to wait. Every time she got distracted—which was about every eight seconds—I jingled her tags. All the leash-shaking I had to do made me wonder if Ella was part sled dog.

By the time we reached Coral Street, I was starting to feel like my old self. I stopped Ella at the curb. I'd left our little block with Ricky before, but never all on my own. I wanted it to be memorable. But I couldn't think of anything special to say. So I looked at Ella the part sled dog, shook her leash, and yelled, "Hyah!"

We hurried across the street and down the block. I felt totally free, like it was just me and Ella on an adventure in the big city—even though we weren't leaving Friendship.

We walked along to Friendship Avenue. I was in such good spirits that I felt like skipping. "But that's just a little too silly, isn't it?" I asked Ella. "After all, we are independent ladies."

Ella and I continued our march toward the park. We passed Atlantic Avenue, and a little while later, we crossed Pacific Avenue. "Look, girl, we went all the way across the country!" I joked.

After a few more blocks, I saw the trees that marked the edge of Friendship Park. We were almost there! The leaves were really starting to come down and I couldn't wait to run Ella through them.

We walked along past a few more houses, but then Ella stopped. I jingled her dog tags. She didn't move. "Come on!" I cried. "Leaf piles and zoomies!"

Ella was standing very strangely. She had turned sideways, facing the street, and one of her front paws just hung in the air, like a hunting dog out of a cartoon.

"What's the matter?" I asked Ella. She didn't seem to hear me. I followed her gaze out past the traffic.

When the cars cleared, I saw it standing across the street. I could barely believe my eyes. Its black and white body was round and plump, and its rear feathers spread around it like a giant duster.

"A wild turkey," I said with almost no sound. The bird stood about Ella's height, with a thin, pink, curved neck and a beak shaped like pliers. I could just barely see its beady, black stare.

Mrs. Okocho had been telling the truth after all. The turkey was just standing by the curb completely out of place, like it had been pulled out of a magician's hat and left behind. It was almost a shame no one else was here to see it, because I had just the word for the moment—*miraculous*.

Then the turkey made a noise. But it wasn't *gobble-gobble*, like you learn about in kindergarten. It was a tough sound, like a bark.

Before I could move a muscle, Ella shot off like a canine cannonball. Like she'd been stuffed with nitroglycerin. She pulled so hard that I toppled over and skinned both of my knees, right through my jeans. The leash slipped off my wrist and Ella was across the street before I could even get to my feet.

"Ella!" I screamed at the top of my lungs.

Ella stopped and looked back as the turkey raced away. Panic rumbled in my stomach and I could feel my nose twitching. I didn't know what else to do, so I pinched my thumb and pointer finger together and waved them quickly. "Teddy Snack!" I shouted. "Ella, Teddy Snack!"

There was still a break in traffic, so I walked as calmly as I could across the street toward my puppy. "Teddy Snack, girl," I said. As I chanted the name of Ella's favorite treat, I waved my hand and prayed that she wouldn't be able to tell that I had nothing to give her.

I was two-thirds across the street when the wild turkey barked again. I screamed my girl's name once more, but this time, Ella was gone.

I hurried up and down every side street in Friendship, calling out Ella's name at each corner. I asked every person I passed if they'd seen her. It was tough, though, because they wanted to know what Ella looked like, and each part of her looked like it came from a different kind of dog.

The hour I was supposed to be gone turned into two. I had to get my little girl back. I had to be the one to find her before she forgot about her chase and realized that she was lost, before she got scared—before she felt as panicked and lonely as I did.

I made my way all the way to the edge of our neighborhood and stopped. Up the hill, I could see the edge of Children's Hospital. It peeked over the tops of the row houses. I'd never really noticed, but tiny lights lined the top of each building, and they changed colors. It looked like a place you'd go to see a play or a concert.

But I knew better than to go there now. I couldn't believe I was even thinking about it. Momma couldn't help me. She would just tell me the same thing that Mr. Harvey had—I should have known better. If she even noticed that I was there.

I turned around to search some more. As I half-ran, half-walked, the streetlights began to flicker on. Friendship Avenue didn't look so friendly anymore.

The bare trees looked like claws and the shadows were dark, deep holes in the ground. My legs burned from all my running. I knew that it would be useless to look more.

When I reached South Graham, I saw blue and red lights flashing ahead. It was the police! They looked like they were out in front of my house. I felt a little hope stir inside of me. Had they found my little Ella and brought her back? I found one last bit of energy and ran all the way home.

As I got closer, I saw a police officer on our front steps. He was talking to Mrs. Okocho… and Momma. Before I could even think, Momma spotted me and sprinted down the steps. She squeezed me so tightly that I could barely breathe. "Oh, God, my baby," she said, her hot tears falling on the top of my head.

It turned out that the police hadn't come about Ella at all. They'd come about me. After I'd left to walk Ella, Ricky had stopped over to apologize again. When Mrs. Okocho learned that I'd sneaked off, she called Momma at work. Then she called the police and raced home to meet them.

"This is going to sting," Momma said. She was about to wipe my skinned knees with peroxide. I nodded, and she went ahead. I hissed, but Momma was gentle and the pain was gone as soon as she took the sterile pad away. I bet she made a great nursing aide.

"Are you going to get in trouble for leaving work early?" I asked.

Momma shook her head and she put a large bandage on each scrape. I stood up for her to look at her work.

"I thought you'd run away," Momma said. "I was sure you'd packed up Ella and run away." Her expression grew angry. "Don't you ever scare me like that again!"

But then she pulled me close and hugged me.

"We have to find Ella, Momma," I said.

"We'll get to work first thing in the morning," she replied. "There's nothing we can do tonight."

A thought came to me. "There is one thing."

Normally, I'm not allowed to stay up past ten o'clock. But tonight, Momma made an exception so that we could make a poster of Ella to hang up around town tomorrow.

I told Momma what it should say, and she typed it up on our computer. We put up Ella's name, our phone number, and at the bottom we added: *Most loved little mutt in the world.*

"Now we just need a picture of her," Momma said.

We opened up the folder that held every picture I'd taken of the puppy since we got her. There were a whole lot of pictures to look through!

"Nope," Momma said, clicking to the next picture. "Nope. Nope."

A whole lot of *blurry* pictures. In one shot she was a red haze trying to climb into our little Christmas tree. In another she was a wagging cloud, eating our Nativity barn. During Momma's birthday in February, she was standing on the couch, her body in perfect focus. But her head was buried inside the sweater I'd gotten Momma as a present.

Momma laughed at that one. "She's such a naughty little girl!"

I smiled in spite of myself. We flipped through some more pictures and got to Ella's birthday. I saw a whirling red blur, surrounded by shredded paper and white fluff. "I remember this one," I said, giggling. "I tried to get her to unwrap her present, that octopus squeaker toy."

"She unwrapped it, all right," Momma said. "She ripped open the paper, then she ripped open the octopus and played with the stuffing!"

We passed the spring and the summer. In the fall photos, we finally found a clear shot. She was lying under the kitchen table, looking up at a spot just above the camera.

"This one's perfect!" Momma said. "When'd we take it?"

"I took it," I answered. A sad feeling rushed up through me and I had to swallow it back. "On meatball hoagie night."

By the time all of the copies of the poster were printed, it was after eleven. "You'd better get to bed, sweetheart," Momma said. "You've had a rough day."

No matter how long I closed my eyes, I couldn't get to sleep. I kept thinking about Ella and how she ought to be curled at the end of my bed, keeping my toes nice and toasty. *She was a stray when we got her*, I thought. *And I made her a stray again.*

I couldn't take it anymore. I climbed out of bed and crept over to Momma's room. "Momma?" I whispered.

Momma rolled over and shifted her covers. "What's wrong, sweetie?" she asked sleepily.

"My feet are cold," I answered. "Can I sleep in here with you?"

Momma slid over in the bed. "Come on in," she said. "I warmed this side up for you."

In the morning, we were startled awake by a loud banging on the door. Momma and I both jumped at the sound. I looked at the clock. It wasn't even seven yet. Momma pulled on her bathrobe and we scrambled to the front door.

Momma yanked open the door to see Mrs. Okocho. "You are not dressed?" she scoffed. "Come now, we have a dog to find!"

I smiled as bright as the sunrise.

I wanted to skip breakfast and just start looking. I felt that if Ella wasn't going to get her Doggy Chow, I shouldn't have any food, either. But Momma made eggs and toast while I was in the shower and basically forced me to eat. The moment I finished, though, she let me and Mrs. Okocho go. Mrs. Okocho had offered to drive me around Friendship to tape up signs. Momma decided to stay home by the phone in case anyone called about Ella.

The Oldsmobile rumbled as Mrs. Okocho and I rode around town. We papered almost every telephone pole in Friendship and then moved on to the neighborhoods around it. "There is a good spot," she said, pointing to the side of a mailbox.

"Are we allowed to tape stuff to a mailbox?" I asked. "It belongs to the government."

"And the government belongs to the people!" Mrs. Okocho declared. "This I learn in my class to be a citizen. Tape away, my girl."

I couldn't really argue with her—partly because I had no idea what she was talking about. There was also something else that I didn't understand. A few more blocks (and a lot of tape) later, I had to ask.

"Mrs. Okocho," I began, "why are you helping me?"

Mrs. Okocho nodded solemnly. "Ella is a very, very bad dog," she said.

I shot her a frustrated stare.

"But," she added, "she gives to you so much love. She is all the time, love, love, love. I cannot let such an animal come to harm."

I wanted to hug Mrs. Okocho, but I couldn't reach her without taking off my seatbelt. I squeezed her arm and hoped she knew what I meant.

A moment later, a frown crossed Mrs. Okocho's face. "That turkey, though," she said, tapping the steering wheel with a disgusted finger. "If I spot that awful beast, I will run it down with all four tires!"

After a few hours, we were all out of posters. There wasn't a chance that anyone could miss them. We decided to head home and wait.

"Thanks so much for helping," I told Mrs. Okocho as we turned onto South Graham Street. "You know, you're one cool elderly lady."

Mrs. Okocho clucked her tongue. "Elderly? Are you crazy, child?" she said. "I am *old*!"

I laughed. I was really lucky to have her around,

silliness and all.

We got a parking spot right near the house. I looked over and saw that Momma was sitting outside on our porch. I knew there must be news, but I was kind of afraid to find out what it was. She didn't look happy or sad. She was just sitting there like a stone.

I hurried to the steps ahead of Mrs. Okocho. "What's up, Momma?" I asked. "Did you hear something?"

Momma sprung to life at the sound of my voice. "Somebody found Ella this morning!" she said quickly.

My heart felt like it was going to jump out of my chest and do a little dance. "Is she upstairs?" I asked.

Momma hesitated. "She's going to be okay," she replied. "She's at Dr. Vanderstam's right now."

"Why is she there?" I demanded. Mrs. Okocho caught up and stood behind me. My eyes kept flitting back and forth between her and Momma. If somebody didn't give me answers, I was ready to scream.

"The woman who found her," Momma began, "she saw the vet's information on the back of Ella's tags and brought her straight there. Sweetie, Ella got hit by a car, maybe last night."

I froze in place. I couldn't open my mouth, or cry, or anything. I didn't know if I'd ever move again.

"Her rear left leg is broken," Momma said. "But she's going to be okay! I talked to Dr. Vanderstam. We need to go over there now. They had to do an operation to try to fix her leg. We should be there when it's done."

CHAPTER NINE

MACK THE KNIFE

Dr. Vanderstam is the tallest, thinnest human being I have ever seen. If he wasn't a vet, I'll bet that he could have been a basketball player. Or maybe the pole that holds up the hoop.

Momma and I were standing with the doctor in an examination room at his clinic. When we first met, I'll be honest—I was a little scared of Dr. Vanderstam. But right now, I was happy that he was like a giant. I don't know why, but it made me feel like he knew all the answers.

Dr. Vanderstam had finished Ella's surgery just before we came. He explained, in his soft, soothing voice, that a kind young woman had found Ella and brought her in just as the clinic was opening. Ella's hind leg had been broken in four places, and her muscles and nerves were hurt, too.

I gripped Momma's hand tightly. "Where is she?" I asked. I wanted to stroke her head and tell her I was sorry.

Dr. Vanderstam pointed behind himself. "She's sleeping," he answered. "We gave her medicine for her pain. It's best to let her rest for now. We don't want to excite her and risk any more injury."

I nodded, feeling a little silly for not thinking of that.

"How did she do in the surgery?" asked Momma. She wrapped her arm around my side.

"As we discussed on the phone, Miss Gandy, Ella's injuries were very complicated," Dr. Vanderstam said. "In the end, I'm sorry to say, we were forced to go with the other option."

Momma put a hand to her cheek. "Poor girl," she whispered.

"What other option?" I asked. Momma hadn't said anything about any options.

Dr. Vanderstam glanced at my mother, like he needed her permission to go on.

I gritted my teeth. "She's *my* dog," I stated, sounding ruder than I'd intended. "What other option?"

Dr. Vanderstam did not seem to be offended. He knelt down to be closer to my height. "I'm very sorry, Latasha," he said. "We had to amputate."

I opened my mouth, but didn't speak. I felt like I knew that word from my dictionary—but I was hoping that I was mixed up.

The kneeling giant furrowed his brow. "We had to remove Ella's leg."

I stamped out into the waiting room. Momma followed me out. "Latasha Esther Gandy," she warned, library-quiet.

"I'll wait out here," I replied, narrowing my eyes into angry slits. "Don't worry. I won't run away."

I thought Momma would yell at me. Instead, she twisted her mouth toward one side of her face like she'd just sucked a lemon. The look in her eyes made me ashamed at how I'd spoken. She backed into the exam room again and closed the door.

I couldn't hold it in anymore. The tears flooded down my cheeks and dripped off the tip of my nose. I was tired of trying to be mature. I was angry, and guilty, and frustrated, and sad, and it felt like each feeling was fighting against the others inside me. I couldn't control any of it. I was so glad that no one else was in the waiting room to see me right then.

No one except for Miss Simon, anyway. She was sitting at the front desk, dressed in her scrubs with a cardigan on top. I didn't want her to see me like this, but there was nowhere to go.

I took a deep breath, hoping that it would help me stay quiet. Instead, I got tears up my nose and let out a loud cough that sounded like a goose honk. I couldn't even cry like a grown-up!

Miss Simon hurried over with a box of tissues. "It's okay, honey," she said, patting my back.

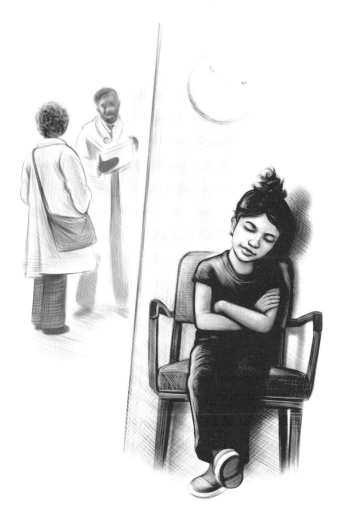

I stabbed a finger at the exam room door. "That creep cut off Ella's leg!" I exclaimed.

Miss Simon looked at me with a smile of sympathy. "Dr. V's a good man," she said. "It's hard to understand now, but this was the best and safest thing to do for Ella. She's going to bounce back and be as good as new."

"Except she won't be," I replied. I wiped my eyes and nose with a tissue. "She'll never be the same."

All because of you, my brain reminded me.

"Well, she'll *look* different," Miss Simon admitted. "But you'd be surprised. When a dog loses a limb, it's very different than when a person does. Once the cut heals and the stitches come out, they pretty much forget they ever had four legs."

Miss Simon had never lied to me before, or even been the least bit dishonest. I wanted to believe her. I wanted to just be glad that Ella was alive and safe. But there was so much I still felt angry about.

"Momma just let him do it," I complained. "She didn't even ask me what I wanted."

Miss Simon nodded in understanding. "Would you really have wanted to make that choice?" she asked.

"No," I confessed.

Miss Simon and I sat quietly beside each other.

"There's actually a saying for times like this," she said. "It goes, 'Dogs aren't born with four legs. They come with three legs and a spare.'"

I looked at her sideways. "Nobody says that," I retorted, determined not to grin.

"Yes, they do," Miss Simon said. "And I think it's true. Dogs are tough. And Ella is the toughest." Miss Simon gave my arm a squeeze. "I'll bet she learned to be tough from her mom."

I gave in and smiled.

"You think you can keep being tough while Ella gets better?" she asked.

I stood up and pointed at the exam room again. "I should go say I'm sorry."

Things were happening almost too fast for me to handle. Less than one day ago, Ella had been my happy, silly pup on a walk. Then she was a runaway, then she got hurt, and then she got saved. And now, we were taking her home.

Dr. Vanderstam's clinic is closed on Sundays. In fact, it's closed after twelve o'clock on Saturdays, but he'd kept it open late just for Ella. He really isn't a creep, not at all. I never should have called him that. He gave us a choice—either check Ella in to the big animal hospital across town for the weekend, or take her home today. That really wasn't a choice at all.

After Momma had filled out all of the paperwork, Miss Simon brought Ella out to us. I squeezed close to Momma's side.

"There's our girl," she whispered.

Ella was still very tired from her medicine. Miss Simon had to wheel her out on a cart. She was lying on it with a blue sheet covering her rear half.

Ella looked like she did when we practiced *take a nap*.

Which is really play dead, I thought. I didn't know if I could be strong like I had to be. I didn't think I could do it at all.

But then Ella caught sight of me. She didn't smile or pant. She didn't get up or try to run over. But her tail…

It started to thump. And whip. And bang. The metal cart rang and the blue sheet jumped like it was alive.

"Settle down, girl," Momma said.

"Shh," said Miss Simon with that voice like a smile.

The sick feeling I'd had since yesterday melted away. I didn't know how Ella could forgive me for losing her. But she had—and to quote a silly, wise, old Nigerian lady, it was *a wonderful*.

Ella's surgery cut was too big to be stitched up. They actually had to close it with staples! Dr. Vanderstam promised me that it didn't hurt more than stitches, but it was a lot stronger and safer.

"And why does she have to wear a lampshade on her head?" I demanded.

"It is a special kind of collar," the doctor explained. "It will keep Ella from licking at her staples and hurting herself."

It still looked like a lampshade to me. And it made

Ella extra tough to carry up the stairs to our apartment. I was glad Momma was there to do it. I was afraid I might catch the big cone-shaped thing on a banister or bump it into the wall.

I hurried into the house and fetched a clean sheet from the closet. I spread it on the couch. We had to make sure that Ella only sat on clean things until her cut healed shut. Momma set her down upon the sheet. Ella stretched sideways and rested her head on the side of her not-a-lampshade collar.

Mrs. Okocho followed us into the living room. "Tell me how else to help," she said.

"You've done more than enough for today," Momma replied.

That was definitely the truth. Mrs. Okocho had driven our family all over town today—and all for a dog she didn't even like much.

Mrs. Okocho turned to me. "I will see you Monday, young lady," she said.

She backed into the kitchen and I heard her close our front door behind her.

"We need to do something really special for her," I said.

Momma smiled. "You're a good kid," she said.

As long as I didn't look at Ella's stapled-up side, I felt like that was true.

That night, Ella refused to eat her Doggy Chow. She wouldn't lift her head for one bite.

"Eat, puppy," I said.

Ella didn't look at me. She just rested her head against her collar on the floor.

"Girl, you have to eat," I instructed. I shouldn't have been upset. Dr. Vanderstam warned us that Ella's pain medicine might take away her appetite. I just thought Ella would be different from all the other dogs. She'd always eaten any food that was offered to her—and a lot of stuff that wasn't offered, too.

"Ella!" I said, my voice growing louder. I knew it was the wrong way to behave, but I still couldn't keep it inside. "If you don't eat, you'll die! Eat your dinner!"

"Latasha," Momma said at the doorway. "Come out here."

I whirled to face her. "Momma, don't you get it?" I pleaded. "She won't eat because of me! I have to make her eat!" I knew that the tears would come next—I could feel them sneaking up behind my eyes.

"Get out here, young lady," Momma ordered. "Right now."

Glancing back at Ella, I slunk over to the doorway.

"You need to listen, and listen good," Momma said.

Listen well, I thought with a sneer.

"It's okay to feel bad about Ella's accident," she continued. "And I'm proud that you want to own up to your part in it."

"There's no *part*," I argued. "It's all my—"

Momma cut me off. "There is a difference between accepting blame," she said, "and feeling sorry for yourself. Now's not the time for feeling sorry. Because it won't help Ella get better. And that's all that matters. Right?"

"Right," I said glumly.

"I mean it," Momma warned. "No panic, no pity parties, no acting grossed out. Remember what Dr. Vanderstam said. Ella will only feel bad if we make her feel bad. We need to make her feel like everything is fine."

I blinked my tears away and nodded. I thought about the long list of tips Dr. Vanderstam and Miss Simon had given us. "They said that if Ella doesn't want to eat normal food, we should make her something special to eat."

"Good thinking," Momma said. "What can we make?"

I thought through the very short list of recipes I knew how to make. "Do we have the stuff to make meatballs?" I asked.

Momma's eyes clicked back and forth as she pictured the ingredients. "We don't have every single thing," she said. "But we can come close enough."

"So we'll make…" The perfect dictionary word popped into my mind. "Makeshift meatballs."

Momma laughed. "Let's do it."

We marched into the kitchen and stood side by side, like a perfect team. "Get ready for a fancy meal," I told Ella. "A fancy meal for a fancy girl."

We scrounged up all the ingredients we could and got to work. We spiced and poured and stirred, and I mixed the raw meat up with my hands. Let me tell you, it wasn't any less icky the second time around.

Momma cooked the meatballs on the stove to save time. While she worked, I entertained Ella by playing a silly word game. I tried to string as many *M* words together in a sentence as I could. I got as far as, "Me and Momma made my mutt a marvelous meal of makeshift meatballs."

Momma set a plate with two cut-up meatballs in front of Ella. The pup inched forward and sniffed. "Feed her a bite," suggested Momma.

I picked up a piece of meatball and held it near Ella's mouth. She craned her neck forward and plucked the piece right out of my hand.

"My good girl!" I cried as Ella licked the juice off my fingertips.

"See?" Momma said, kneeling down beside me. "Just fine."

By bedtime, everything almost did feel fine. Ella was back at the end of my bed, like normal. But there was one cool change I'd made. I had moved my mattress off my bed frame and onto the floor. That way, Ella would not fall and get hurt if she tried to move in the middle of the night. Momma thought it was a very smart idea.

"This is pretty fun, huh?" I asked. Ella was still very sleepy and weak, but I tried to be as cheery as could be. "It's like we're out camping!"

My eyes kept wandering down to Ella's lower half. I made myself look at the huge cut where Ella's leg used to be. The area around it was shaved clean of fur. The cut was stapled and bruised and ugly red.

Not ugly, I told myself. I tried to think of a thing I liked that the cut reminded me of. The best I could come up with was Halloween.

"I was thinking," I told Ella. "Maybe we can be pirates together. I can wear an eye-patch, and you can have a peg leg." She peered past the edge of her big collar, as if to say, *Yeah right*. "Well, it's either that or Frankenstein, pup."

Ella Frankenstein Gandy, I thought. *Ella Frankenstein Lampshade Head Gandy.*

Ella tried to shift her body and she whimpered in pain. She must have pulled on her staples a little. I sat up and petted her shoulders. "It's okay, girl," I whispered. "You're not Ella Frankenstein. You'll always be my little Ella Fitzgerald."

Ella looked at me with sad, confused eyes. She really didn't understand what had happened to her. She just knew that she hurt. I looked around the room for something I could use to distract her—a chew toy or a rope or a secret stash of Teddy Snacks. All I could see from the floor was the stack of unread Book Mountain books on my desk.

Then something clicked in my brain.

"Once upon a time," I said suddenly. "Once upon a time, there was this lady named Ella. Pretty nice name, huh? Actually, her name was Ella Fitzgerald, just like you!"

I scratched at my girl's neck underneath her weird collar.

"And just like you, Ella was beautiful," I went on. "She had a beautiful voice. She was a singer. And she was famous all over the world. Everyone wanted to hear her.

"One night, she was doing a concert in a huge concert hall. After every song, the crowd clapped 'til their hands hurt. It was going perfectly until Ella got to this one song. Its name was 'Mack the Knife.'

"Ella sang part of the song, but then, right in the middle of it all, the worst thing happened. She forgot the words! Can you believe it?"

I stared at my girl with wide eyes.

"Ella forgot the words. There were a couple of ways she could have handled it. She could have given up

and stopped the song. She could have run off the stage, totally ashamed, and let it wreck the whole night. But that's not what she did. Not at all.

"Do you know what Ella did?" I asked. "She just made up new words! She made up a whole new set of words to sing, right on the spot. And you know what? The new song was fun, funny, and better than that real old 'Mack the Knife' any day of the week.

"That's why Ella Fitzgerald is my favorite singer," I went on. "And that's how you got your name. So you see, Ella, you've got no choice."

I stretched back and pulled my covers up to my neck. "You have to get better," I said. "You're not allowed to quit. Ella Fitzgeralds never quit."

Before I turned out my nightlight, I peeked toward my feet and smiled. Ella had drifted off to sleep.

CHAPTER TEN
ALL THE WAY BACK

I'd like to be able to say that after the first night, there was no more frustration and no more tears. But that just wouldn't be honest. Sometimes, Ella seemed like she was her same old self and we both felt great. But other times, she seemed almost like she was some other dog—a dog that had watched Ella very closely and tried hard to act just like her, but couldn't get it quite right. Those were the times that made me hurt inside.

I can say this, though—my girl was no quitter. Each day, she got a little stronger. Each day, she gave me a new reason to feel proud of her.

On Sunday, she took her first steps by herself. To be more exact, Ella wandered out of my bedroom before I woke up, scaring me half to death. I found her in the kitchen, staring at the box of Teddy Snacks on the counter.

On Monday, she had enough strength to walk all the way around the apartment. Her new walk was kind of awkward. She took a step with each of her front paws, then hopped forward with her rear leg. She looked like she was part dog, part pogo-stick.

The next day, she figured out how to wag her tail without tipping herself over. By the end of the week, she was able to sit and give paw.

Ella wasn't the only one who made me proud. Mrs. Okocho surprised me, too. While Ella was getting better, she actually offered to come upstairs and watch me. That way I could give my pup the extra care she needed. Of course, Mrs. Okocho grumbled about climbing the stairs. And she washed her hands with soap every time Ella so much as breathed on them. But I think she got a kick out of seeing Ella slowly get better.

Momma was such a big help. She spent time with us every evening after she got home. Work still tired her out, but she always checked on Ella's staples and made sure the cut was clean. And she checked on me, too. I don't think Momma realized before how lonely I had been feeling without her around. But I told her about it, and now Momma always made sure to ask about any good news from the day, and any worries I had.

After I put on my pajamas, though, it was just my girl and me. Ella and I camped out on my floor-bed, and I read her storybooks until she found just the right way to lie down and sleep comfortably. Sometimes I read to her even after she fell asleep, because I think the sound of my voice helped her to have good dreams.

All that reading actually had a double purpose. It was good for Ella, but it also counted for Book Mountain.

I should explain what happened. On the Monday after Ella's accident, we started the day with silent reading time. I was so tired from the weekend that I had a hard time keeping my eyes open. So when Mr. Harvey called me out in the hall, I figured I was going to get in trouble for dozing off. But that wasn't it at all.

"Ricky came to me this morning," Mr. Harvey said. "He told me the truth about this book report business."

I glanced toward the classroom—somehow I'd actually forgotten that I was mad at that kid.

"I owe you an apology," he said. "On Friday, I should have given you a chance to defend yourself. Instead, I flew off the handle."

I thought about the last few days I'd had. "It's really hard to be mature sometimes," I said heavily.

Mr. Harvey smiled. "You've got that right, Latasha," he said. "Anyway, Ricky is still out for Book Mountain. He cheated, and I can't ignore that. But if you want back in, you're welcome to rejoin us. We're awfully close to the lead, you know. We could use your help."

And so every night I read to Ella, and I wrote up the summaries at the benches during lunch. I didn't have much time for my pocket dictionary on those days, but I did take a glance sometimes when I needed a break. In fact, I found a great word to describe my dog—*pugilist*. It means *fighter*. That was Ella to the letter.

Soon it was Halloween. Ella wasn't ready to go trick-or-treating, but we wore costumes around the house anyway. I wore the monster mask I'd made in art class. For Ella, Mrs. Okocho made some drawings of her garden. Then I colored the drawings in and taped them to the inside of Ella's lampshade collar. Her costume was "bouquet of flowers."

It was a pretty good costume, even though Ella ended up pulling off one of the pictures with her teeth and eating it. Guess which picture she ate? The one of Mrs. Okocho's daisies. Really, I should have seen it coming.

At school the day after Halloween, the results were in. Dr. DeSoto, our principal, told the whole school during morning announcements.

"And the winner of this year's Book Mountain is… Mr. Harvey's third grade!"

Our whole class screamed and whooped in excitement. Mr. Harvey pretended like the sound was knocking him back against the chalkboard.

"Congratulations," Dr. DeSoto declared. "Your pizza party will happen this Friday, so pick out your favorite toppings!"

I could swear I heard Dante Preston licking his lips.

Friday, November fourth, was more than just pizza day. It was also the fourteenth day since Ella's surgery. It was time to bring her to the vet, and if Dr. Vanderstam said she was okay, my puppy could get her staples out!

Momma took half of the day off so that we could bring her in right after school. At first I was really worried about Momma taking any time off. Ella's surgery had been very expensive. I was scared that

Momma would get fired for skipping work and that we wouldn't be able to make the payments.

"Relax, sweetie," she said. "I didn't just skip out. I traded some hours with one of the other aides. I'll make them up some time next week."

"You can do that?" I asked.

"Of course," Momma said. "If it's really important, I can always find time."

We had our pizza party during the last period of the day as a nice way to end the week. There was a whole stack of pizza boxes and a bunch of two-liter pop bottles on Mr. Harvey's desk. We took turns getting our plates ready with two slices of pizza for each of us.

On my way up to the front, I noticed Ricky's empty seat. Our teacher had kept his word—Ricky had to miss out on the pizza and pop. Instead, he had to go wait for the final bell in a place called In-School-Suspension.

I picked out a slice of green pepper pizza and a slice of pepperoni and had Mr. Harvey pour me a 7-Up. Then I asked him for a favor.

I opened the door to In-School-Suspension and went in. I had to hold the 7-Up cup in my teeth to get the door open. Different teachers kept watch over the room at different times. Right then, it was our gym teacher, Miss Schneider. I showed her my hall pass.

Ricky lifted his head off his desk at the sight of me. "Latasha?" he asked.

"You want green pepper or pepperoni?" I replied.

"Pepperoni!" he said.

"Too bad," I said with a wince. "I already called it."

I sat down in the empty seat next to him. "Green pepper's fine," he said. "How'd you get Mr. Harvey to let you down here?"

"I asked."

Ricky nodded as if it was some kind of genius idea he'd never thought of. We each took a bite of our pizza. While we ate, we caught up.

"I heard about Ella," Ricky said. "I'm really sorry."

"She's going to be okay," I said. I told him a little about all of her hard work the past two weeks.

"How'd she get away from you, anyway?" he asked, taking another bite.

When I told him what had happened, Ricky almost choked on his pizza.

"The turkey was real?!" he gasped, coughing.

I waited while Ricky caught his breath. He took a sip of pop. "I wanted to make Ella a card or something," he said, wiping his eyes with a napkin. "Not a store card—a homemade one. But all my ideas were dumb. The best I could come up was… 'Get well-a, Ella!'"

I laughed. "That would've been awesome," I said. "Just come by and say hi to her soon."

Ricky nodded.

I held up my pizza crust. "You want this?" I asked.

"Why are you being so nice now?" asked Ricky.

"What? I only like the crust at Pizza Franco."

"You know what I mean," he responded. "What happened?"

I shrugged. "For one, it's really not fun to be mad at your friend," I explained. "And, I never did give you back that basketball from the summer."

"You still have that?" he asked.

"Plus…"

"Plus what?"

"Well," I said. "Ella's almost back to normal. I thought that if we made up… maybe she'd go all the way back to normal."

Ricky thought it over. "Yep, you're still pretty odd," he said with a grin. He held up his own pizza crust. "Want to play swordfight?"

After school, Mrs. Okocho's car rolled up to the curb. But she wasn't alone. In the front seat was Momma. She was holding Ella in her lap.

Ricky pointed at Ella's collar. "Wow, she looks like a bullhorn!" he said, which got him an elbow in the ribs.

"See you later, turkey," I said.

We drove straight over to the vet clinic. Dr. Vanderstam gave Ella a full check-up. When he was done, he had great news! Ella's scar was fully healed.

"What do you say we take those pesky staples out?" he asked.

"And the lampshade?" I asked.

The vet chuckled. "That can come off, too."

After Dr. Vanderstam was finished, Mrs. Okocho drove us home. Ella rode in my lap on the way back. She was so much easier to hold without that ridiculous collar. At one point, we hit a pothole and my hand brushed Ella's scar. It felt a little bumpy, but now that the staples were gone, it wasn't really scary at all.

Once we got home, Momma and Ella climbed the flight up to our apartment. I stayed down with Mrs. Okocho and watched. Ella was a lot more nervous on stairs than she used to be, but she made it all the way to the top without any help.

"That's my pretty little pugilist!" I called up as they entered the apartment.

Mrs. Okocho tapped me on the shoulder. "What are you waiting for?" she asked. "Go play with your little girl."

"Actually," I replied. "There's something I wanted to ask you. Can I come in?"

Mrs. Okocho let me into her apartment and led me into the dining room. "What is it, my dear?" she asked.

"You've been so great this whole time, Mrs. Okocho," I said. "I wanted to know something. If you're not busy… do you want to come have Thanksgiving with us this year?"

Excitement spread across Mrs. Okocho's face. I was nervous that she would pinch my cheek out of sheer joy, but she didn't. Her eyes just began to glisten. "I would like nothing more," she replied, her voice cracking. She cleared her throat. "But on one condition."

"Sure," I said.

"You really must let me cook something!"

I rubbed my mouth with my hand. It was all I could do to hold back a groan. Why did everything always backfire on me?

Even the room seemed disappointed. The ceiling began to rumble and the walls began to rattle. As the chandelier shook, Mrs. Okocho looked up and gave a weary sigh. "It never ends," she said, shaking her head.

I ran out to the hall and up the stairs. I threw open our front door and rushed inside. I turned just in time to see a red furball rush in and out of the kitchen.

The zoomies.

"Ella, no!" yelled Momma from the living room.

I went to the kitchen doorway and watched my Ella on the rampage. She sent our furniture sheets flying and bumped the magazines off the coffee table. I smiled wide as the tripod tornado ripped from room to room.

She wasn't quite as fast, and I knew she'd tire out very soon. But without a doubt, my naughty, happy little April Fool was all the way back. I didn't care one bit about Momma's dog switch. It could wait 'til tomorrow, or it could wait forever.

"Ella Fitzgerald Gandy," I stated. But it wasn't a warning, and it wasn't a threat—not today.

It was just a fact.

THE END